"I needed the time away from you."

There was frustration and anger in the dark depths of his eyes as he moved toward her, then closed his hands around her upper arms.

"Do you have any idea how crazy you make me? One minute I'm certain you care, and the next you're as cold as ice. I tell myself not to think about you, and yet you haunt my dreams." His hands tightened their hold. "Look me in the eyes, Laura, and tell me one last time you don't give a damn about me. Make me believe it."

She ordered herself to say it. But her chin trembled, and the words stuck in her throat.

"Laura?" he said softly. "You don't have to be afraid of me."

She tried to speak. She wanted to tell him coolly that she didn't care—that she wasn't afraid of him. But the lie was too great. The truth was that she *did* care—and that terrified her.

Dear Reader,

Welcome to Silhouette—experience the magic of the wonderful world where two people fall in love. Meet heroines that will make you cheer for their happiness, and heroes (be they the boy next door or a handsome, mysterious stranger) who will win your heart. Silhouette Romance reflects the magic of love—sweeping you away with books that will make you laugh and cry, heartwarming, poignant stories that will move you time and time again.

In the coming months we're publishing romances by many of your all-time favorites, such as Diana Palmer, Brittany Young, Sondra Stanford and Annette Broadrick. Your response to these authors and our other Silhouette Romance authors has served as a touchstone for us, and we're pleased to bring you more books with Silhouette's distinctive medley of charm, wit and—above all—*romance*.

I hope you enjoy this book and the many stories to come. Experience the magic!

Sincerely,

Tara Hughes
Senior Editor
Silhouette Books

ELIZABETH AUGUST

Something So Right

Published by Silhouette Books New York
America's Publisher of Contemporary Romance

To my three sons—
Douglas, Benjamin, and Matthew—
for conducting their disputes in lowered voices
and keeping the television and stereo
at less than mind-boggling volume
so that I could finish this book.

SILHOUETTE BOOKS
300 E. 42nd St., New York, N.Y. 10017

ISBN: 0-373-08668-7

First Silhouette Books printing August 1989

Printed in the U.S.A.

Books by Elizabeth August

Silhouette Romance

Author's Choice #554
Truck Driving Woman #590
Wild Horse Canyon #626
Something So Right #668

ELIZABETH AUGUST

lives in Wilmington, Delaware, with her husband, Doug, and her three boys, Douglas (15), Benjamin (11) and Matthew (6). She began writing romances soon after Matthew was born. She'd always wanted to write.

Elizabeth does Counted-cross Stitching to keep from eating at night. It doesn't always work. "I love to bowl, but I'm not very good. I keep my team's handicap high. I like hiking in the Shenandoahs as long as we start up the mountain so that the return trip is down rather than vice-versa." She loves to go to Cape Hatteras to watch the sun rise over the ocean.

Elizabeth August has also published books under the pseudonym Betsy Page.

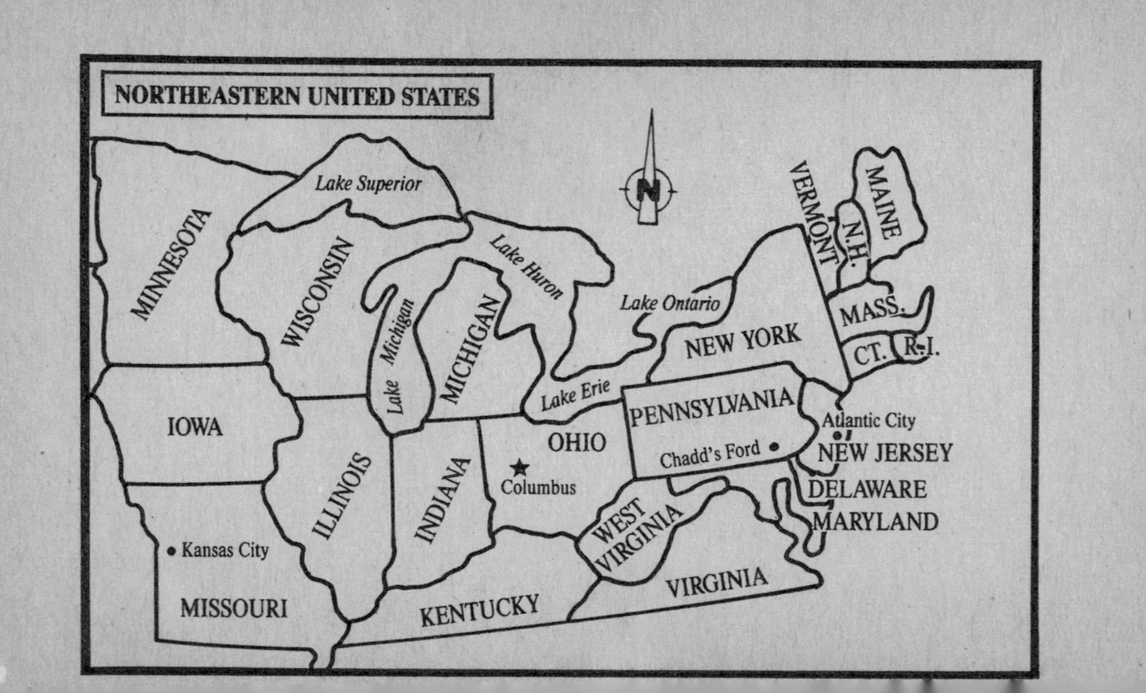
NORTHEASTERN UNITED STATES
N
Lake Superior
MINNESOTA
WISCONSIN
Lake Michigan
MICHIGAN
Lake Huron
Lake Ontario
Lake Erie
VERMONT
N.H.
MAINE
MASS.
CT.
R.I.
NEW YORK
PENNSYLVANIA
Chadd's Ford
Atlantic City
NEW JERSEY
DELAWARE
MARYLAND
IOWA
ILLINOIS
INDIANA
OHIO
Columbus
WEST VIRGINIA
VIRGINIA
KENTUCKY
Kansas City
MISSOURI

Chapter One

Laura Martin faced Frank Davidson grimly. "My brother is not a thief!" she stated unequivocally.

Remaining seated behind his desk, Frank studied the woman glaring down at him. Ted had always described his sister as cute, with a look of vulnerability that masked a will of iron. Frank could see the will of iron in the icy brown eyes. And, in spite of her efforts to hide it, she *was* cute. The conservatively tailored gray suit and high-necked, cream-colored silk blouse she wore didn't completely hide the very feminine curves of her body. Also adding a starkness to her appearance, her long chestnut hair was pulled tightly back into a chignon at the nape of her neck in a severe, spinsterly fashion. But her large brown eyes, full lips and small nose negated the harshness of the hairstyle.

However, he did fail to see any vulnerability. She reminded him of a she cat protecting her young. He drew a tired breath. He was in no mood for this confrontation. Shoving his chair away from the paper-cluttered desk in front of him, he said with dismissal, "The evidence against your brother is fairly complete. Now if you will excuse me, I've got a business to run." The scowl on his face deepened as he added grimly, "What's left of it."

Laura Martin hadn't spent two full hours building up her courage to face Frank Davidson to allow him to put her off so easily. Standing her ground, she continued to glare at the man. Ted had said the ladies found Frank appealing. Admittedly, he did have an interesting face, and his thick black hair, worn a little on the shaggy side, gave him a roguishly handsome appearance. His eyes were as dark as his hair and shuttered like those of a man who kept his innermost thoughts to himself. As he rose, she judged him to be about six feet two inches tall. His blue broadcloth shirt fitted comfortably across sturdy shoulders, and his abdomen was flat. As her gaze continued down over the faded jeans that fit snugly around his muscular thighs to his hand-tooled leather cowboy boots, she conceded that he would be considered attractive by the major portion of the female population. But those dark eyes of his made her feel uneasy, and she found his hardheadedness singularly unappealing.

Returning her gaze to his face, she found him watching her with a quizzically raised eyebrow as if to ask if she liked what she saw. Arrogant in addition to being bullheaded, she mused, and the scowl on her face deepened. "Ted was framed."

"It's been a long day, lady, and I've still got to check the plugs in one of my trucks," he said curtly. "If you honestly believe what you're telling me, you should be talking to the police."

Stepping in front of the door, she blocked his exit. "I have talked to the police and I've talked to Ted's lawyer. Neither one of them was encouraging." She drew a breath. "You're the last person I would choose to come to for help, but I'm desperate. You're right, the evidence against my brother is strong, but he's innocent."

Hooking his thumbs in the pockets of his jeans, Frank impatiently regarded the woman in front of him. He knew a little about her. She was twenty-seven, even though she looked more like twenty, she was not married and she worked as a secretary for a large company in Kansas City, Missouri. Her mother had had cancer and she'd taken care of her until Evelyn Martin had died two years ago. Her father had died of a heart attack several years earlier, which made Ted the only close family Laura had left. He admired her loyalty even if it was misplaced. "They found one of the TV sets from the last stolen shipment in his apartment, and a shoe box with over fifteen thousand dollars in it hidden in his closet," he pointed out.

"Ted swears he doesn't know how the television set or the money got into his apartment. He didn't even know they were there. The money was well hidden, and the television was one of those little portable things and it was stashed behind a chair." But even as she argued her brother's case, Laura knew it was a losing battle. Frank Davidson's expression remained cold. Her jaw tightened. "He admired you," she said in a tone that implied she questioned her brother's judgment. "He thought you were his friend as well as his boss. He's worked for you for nearly a year and a half now. You should know he's not a thief."

"All I know is that I've had several trucks hijacked. My insurance company is threatening to drop me, and my customers are finding new haulers." His gaze narrowed on her challengingly. "If he was innocent, why'd he run when the police came by to talk to him?"

"Because he knew they weren't there just to talk," she snapped. The cool, composed facade she was attempting to maintain threatened to collapse as her frustration built. She'd been through this with the police and with Ted's lawyer. It had been an effort in futility and from the way Frank Davidson was staring at her coldly, she knew he wasn't going to listen to her, either. Still she had to try. "He had just entered his apartment Tuesday when he received an anonymous tip that the police were outside waiting to arrest him. I'm sure it was the same anonymous caller who phoned the police and pointed them in Ted's direction. *And*, I'm equally certain the caller was the person who stashed the money and television set in Ted's apartment. Anyway, when Ted hung up, he didn't really believe the caller but he went and looked out the window. Sure enough there were plainclothes and uniformed men approaching the house. He panicked. You know Ted. He doesn't always act rationally."

"Fifteen thousand dollars is a lot of money to use to simply frame someone," Frank pointed out, the tone of his voice saying he wasn't buying this explanation. "A third of that amount would've been sufficient."

Laura's lips formed a hard, straight line. It had been a long day. She told herself to leave before she said something she would regret, but she was too upset to obey. "I should've known coming here would be useless. They always say you can tell who your real friends are when you're down and out. My brother thought you were his friend." She raked Frank Davidson with an icy gaze. "Clearly he was very mistaken." Tossing him a final cutting glare, she stalked out of the office.

She was making her way across the gravel parking area when fingers like steel closed around her arm. The heat of the contact startled her. It seemed to burn into her, trailing fire up her arm.

Jerking her to a halt, Frank scowled into her face. "For the past twelve years, I've worked day and night to build this business. Now I'm holding on by the skin of my teeth. I liked your brother. I trusted him. Now

I don't know who to trust.'' Releasing her as abruptly as he'd caught her, he strode away.

As she watched his departing back, the ice in her eyes melted a little. Though he'd made her angry, she felt a sympathy for him. Her brother had always talked about how hard Frank Davidson worked and not just for himself. Ted had told her that Frank's parents owned a small farm in Ohio, and Frank had helped them through some pretty lean times in addition to putting his younger brother and sister through college. She could understand his frustration but that didn't give him the right to prejudge Ted! Turning away sharply, she continued toward Ted's car.

Driving to the hospital, she wondered what she would tell her brother. She wanted to be encouraging, but she didn't want to lie to him. The problem was there wasn't anything encouraging to say.

Entering Ted's room, she again said a grateful prayer that he was alive, though she wasn't certain how. Ted rented the top floor of an old farmhouse near Chadds Ford, Pennsylvania. When the police knocked on his front door, he'd run out the back and taken off across country on his dirt bike. But the police had called in a helicopter for the pursuit. The chase had ended when Ted crashed in a ravine. Now he was in a hospital bed with both legs and one arm in traction, several broken ribs and cuts and abrasions over his face and arms, but no irreparable damage.

''You look tired,'' he said, watching her cross the room.

His chestnut hair and brown eyes matched hers. He was only two years younger than her but she'd always thought of him as her *kid* brother because, while she'd grown up taking life very seriously, he'd always looked for the fun. But he was a good kid and had never gotten into any real trouble until now. "I am," she admitted, giving him a light kiss on the cheek before sinking into the chair beside the bed.

"Didn't have much luck, did you?" he asked with a worried frown.

She took his hand in hers. "You shouldn't have run."

"I know," he admitted. "But I was scared. I thought if I could stay free, I could clear myself."

She shook her head. "You've been watching too much television."

He gave her a crooked smile, then his expression again became serious. "Did you talk to Frank?"

Her jaw tensed as she thought of the dark-eyed trucker. "I talked to him."

"No good, huh?" Disappointment was strong on Ted's face. "I thought he might be willing to listen to my side. The doc told me he paced the waiting room for hours Tuesday evening until he was certain I was going to be all right."

Although Frank had left the hospital by the time Laura arrived Wednesday morning, he'd been the one to call her and tell her about Ted's accident, and she remembered the anxiousness in his voice. That was one of the reasons she'd actually gotten up the courage to go talk to him. Now she wondered why she'd bothered. "He was probably worried you would die before you could tell the police who the other gang members were," she said cynically.

"I admit I was angry, but I'm not cold-blooded."

Startled by the intrusion of the icy male voice, Laura jerked her attention toward the door to find Frank Davidson entering the room. He was still dressed as he had been when she'd seen him a little earlier, only now there was a grease smear across one cheek. He must have been in the middle of working on a truck when he'd decided to come to the hospital. Obviously he'd acted on the decision immediately.

Approaching the bed, he stood on the side opposite from her and stared down at Ted as if trying to read his thoughts. "It doesn't make any sense for a bunch of crooks to use fifteen thousand dollars for a frame," he said curtly.

A thought that had been nagging at Laura grew even stronger. It was a long shot, but she was desperate. "It would if the thieves weren't simply after a profit," she said levelly. "Maybe running you out of business is more important to them than cashing in on the loot. Maybe they were worried the police might be getting close to the truth. They framed my brother so the investigation would concentrate on him and his associates."

Frank shifted his scowl from Ted to her.

The intensity of his gaze made her uneasy, but she refused to show it. "Surely, with as winning a personality as you have, you must have made a few enemies," she finished dryly.

A self-derisive smile played at the corners of his mouth. "I've made a few," he admitted. Then turning his attention back to Ted, he demanded harshly, "You going to stick to your story?"

"It's the truth," Ted replied.

For a long moment, Frank regarded him narrowly, then he shook his head. "I'd like to believe you. But other lines have been hit. Not as hard as me, but they've been hit."

"Like Ted, those robberies could be smoke screens," Laura interjected, not willing to give up her theory too easily.

"I suppose it's something to think about," Frank admitted gruffly, then, after nodding a terse goodbye to both of them, he strode out of the room.

"He's almost as civilized as a barbarian but not quite," Laura mused sarcastically as the door swung shut behind the man.

"Frank's not so bad," Ted said, defending Frank. "He's just worried. He's got a lot to lose."

"You're right," she conceded, again feeling an unexpectedly strong surge of sympathy for the trucker.

"And he did come by," Ted continued thoughtfully. "Maybe he's not so certain of my guilt after all."

"Maybe," she agreed hopefully. Then still seriously considering the idea that someone had a vendetta against Frank Davidson, she asked, "Do you know anyone who'd want to ruin him?"

Ted shook his head. "He's not always an easy man to get along with, but he's a fair one. 'Course there are a lot of hotheads in this business. He could've crossed one of them. But I wouldn't know...."

Later that night, lying in bed in Ted's apartment, Laura continued to consider the possibility of a vendetta against Frank Davidson. She thought about going back to the police and telling them about her idea but they hadn't been too receptive toward her the first time. They had a heavy caseload and no extra manpower to chase down unfounded theories. Besides, they were certain Ted was guilty. What she needed was a solid suspect or two to present them with. Frowning up at the ceiling, she remembered the Twenty-Four Hours Café. She'd never been there but Ted mentioned it constantly during his infrequent visits. It was near Frank Davidson's place and catered to truckers. According to Ted, the food wasn't that good but the clientele all knew one another, which gave it a comfortable atmosphere. "Besides, it's a real taste of home for me," Ted had joked. "Their food tastes a lot like your cooking."

She smiled at the remembered boyish mischievousness in his eyes when he'd said it. Then he'd asked for a third helping of her stew. Her hands balled into fists. She just couldn't let Ted go to jail. She knew it was an outside chance that she might hear something that would help her brother if she went to the café, but she was willing to take it. She had to do something! Tomorrow morning she would have breakfast at the Twenty-Four Hours Café.

Satisfied that she had a plan of action, no matter how futile, she closed her eyes and slept.

The next morning, wanting to blend in with the rest of the crowd, Laura dressed in jeans, sneakers and a lightweight sweater. She let her hair hang long and tied it back with a blue bandanna. Briefly she considered wearing a bit more makeup than the very light touch she normally wore, then decided against that. She wanted to blend in, not attract attention.

Hoping no one would notice Ted's car and recognize it, she parked in the back between a couple of very large trucks. A May breeze still carrying the hint of the winter's chill whisked around her as she hurried toward the café. Inside, the eatery was long and narrow, with a row of booths on the windowed side. Across from the booths was a line of stools along the full length of a counter facing the grill. Choosing an end booth, Laura ordered coffee, eggs and bacon. She'd brought in a newspaper and feigned great interest in it while she listened to the conversations around her.

As she had suspected, the major portion of the talk was about the robberies, but what she heard, she didn't like. Most of the customers seemed to think Ted was guilty. Those who didn't feel that way weren't offering any alternative suspects. For nearly three-quarters of an hour she sat there, her frustration growing stronger by the minute. Reaching the conclusion that this was not going to help Ted, she was just getting ready to leave when she heard a chorus of welcoming shouts.

"Hey, Frank," a robust looking customer greeted the newly arriving patron. "Ain't seen you in here in a dog's age. Thought maybe Mabel's cooking finally ate through your stomach."

"Don't look like it's been bothering you none," a gray-haired woman yelled out from behind the grill, and several of the customers laughed good-naturedly, including the robust man.

Laura paled as Frank Davidson entered the café. The last thing she wanted was to be recognized. No one was going to talk to her or let anything slip in front of her if they knew she was Ted's sister. Quickly putting her newspaper up in front of her, she cautiously peered around it to watch Frank exchange nods of greeting with several of the other customers as he strode toward a booth in her direction. To her chagrin he chose the one next to hers. The only saving grace was that he sat down with his back toward her.

The blond waitress who had waited on her approached Frank's table with a welcoming smile. "You shouldn't be such a stranger," she chided flirtatiously, whipping out her order book and thumbing to an empty page.

"Forgot how nice the scenery was here," Frank replied in an easy drawl.

"Well, you just better come and look more often," the waitress returned with an inviting wink and a little shift of her hips.

Watching the exchange Laura suddenly felt the bile rise in her throat. "I guess some men need variety," she remembered her mother saying bitterly. The scene that had flashed uninvited into her mind had taken place over twelve years ago but it was as vivid to her as if it had happened only yesterday. She recalled the pain in her mother's eyes, and the anger Laura had felt swept over her once again. Stunned that such a simple exchange could cause such painful memories to surface, she scowled at herself. How Frank Davidson lived his private life meant nothing to her. Unless it could provide a clue to a new suspect for the robberies, she amended.

Frank ordered his food and the waitress swung her hips a little as she moved away from his table.

A lean man sitting at the counter turned to face Frank. "Heard Hayes was going to give you one more shot at getting some of that special equipment of his through."

"Yeah, I'm running it myself," Frank answered, adding grimly, "those thieves try to take this one, they'll have to deal with me personally."

Rambo couldn't have said it better, Laura thought sarcastically.

"Who you going to take with you to ride shotgun?" a heavyset man at a nearby table asked.

"No one," Frank replied. "I don't trust anyone but myself any more."

"Right shame about Ted Martin," the blond waitress said, returning to pour Frank some coffee. "He was kinda cute. Too bad he turned out bad."

For the umpteenth time Laura bit her bottom lip to hold back a protest. She'd come here to help her brother, and a shouting match in this truckers' hangout wasn't going to do that.

"Never knew our local paper could hold anyone's attention for so long," a male voice abruptly interrupted Laura's thoughts.

She'd been concentrating so hard on Frank she hadn't noticed the tall, blond-haired man approach her table. Looking up, she saw a pair of deep blue, smiling eyes. From his dress, she guessed he was probably a trucker, too. He had sort of a Robert Redford look about him, and the confident expression on his face suggested he was used to being well received by the ladies. If Frank hadn't been sitting at the next table she might have been tempted to invite the man to join her and see what she could learn from him. But she couldn't very well quiz him now.

"I'm meeting someone," she replied with a note of dismissal. Frank's shoulders straightened, and she experienced a sinking feeling in the pit of her stomach.

"You've been here a right long time," the man noted in a friendly drawl, clearly not willing to give up so easily. "Be a shame for a pretty thing like you to be stood up. How about letting me join you and show that boyfriend of yours how dangerous it is to leave you stranded for so long?''

Frank glanced over his shoulder. As his dark gaze leveled on her, Laura held her breath waiting for him to expose her. But he remained silent and turned his attention back to his own table. Now that he'd seen her, she had no reason to linger. In fact, the sooner she left the better off she'd be. ''I'm not meeting him here. I was just a little early so I stopped here for breakfast and some coffee. Now I need to be going.''

The man continued to regard her with a lazy grin. ''If you'd been meeting me, you could've come by as early as you wanted.''

''Maybe some other time,'' she replied with a quick, flirtatious smile. While she had no desire to spend a moment with this man, he might have some information. If nothing else turned up, she wanted to be able to talk to him.

''Name's Joe Monroe,'' he said. ''I'm in the phone book. You just call anytime, pretty lady.''

Silently praying it wouldn't be necessary, she continued to smile plastically. ''Thanks. I'll keep that in mind.'' Picking up her check, she eased out of the booth past Joe. As she made her way to the cash register, the hairs on the back of her neck prickled, and glancing over her shoulder she saw Frank watching her. There was nothing friendly in his gaze. Quickly paying her bill, she left.

She had just reached Ted's car when a familiar steellike grip closed around her arm. Turning, she found herself looking into Frank's dark, suspicious eyes.

"Who are you meeting?" he demanded.

Again the heat of his touch disconcerted her. It spread up her arm, and she found herself acutely aware of his masculinity. Telling herself this was strictly an overreaction eaused by her taut nerves, she tried to jerk free but his hold remained strong. Stopping the struggle, she faced him levelly. "I'm not meeting anyone. It was just an excuse to get out of there."

The suspicion in his eyes grew stronger. "And why were you there in the first place?"

Her chin tilted defiantly. "I was there trying to find out something that could help my brother."

The grip on her arm tightened. "Look, lady, I'm in no mood for games. If Ted sent you to meet someone, I want to know who."

An angry flush spread over Laura's face. "You think I was trying to make contact with a crook?"

"You're trying to help your brother, and he's mixed up in some pretty bad business," Frank replied grimly. "It's my guess you'd meet with just about anyone to help him. But the only way you're going to really help him is to get him to tell the truth."

Laura's eyes glistened with fury. "He is telling the truth, and if you don't let go of me this minute, I'm going to start screaming."

Frank's jaw tensed. Slowly, he released her. "If you're telling me the truth, then you're only looking for trouble. Leave the investigating to the police. You could get yourself hurt."

"The police are investigating the wrong people," she snapped. "I'm not going to sit by idly and watch my brother be railroaded into prison for something he didn't do!"

Frank raked a hand through his hair in an agitated manner. "Take my advice. Go visit your brother, talk to the police, talk to Ted's lawyer. If you want to, hire a private detective. But stay out of this personally and stay away from men like Joe Monroe."

Interest sparked in her eyes. Were Frank and Joe enemies? "What's wrong with Joe Monroe?"

"He's the kind of man who'll promise you the moon to get you into his bed and the next morning he'll be gone and you'll have nothing," he growled.

Again the bile rose in her throat. "You don't have to warn me about the fickleness of men," she hissed, then wished she'd bitten her tongue. She'd let the bitterness she normally kept well hidden show, and Frank was studying her with curiosity. She met his inspection with cool dignity. "Now if you'll excuse me, I've got to come up with a way to clear my brother."

"Ted did once tell me you could be real bullheaded," he muttered.

She smiled dryly. "Takes one to know one," she replied and climbing into the car, drove off.

Chapter Two

Driving away from the Twenty-Four Hours Café, Laura glanced in the rearview mirror and saw Frank Davidson standing where she'd left him. Frowning at herself, she couldn't believe she'd lost her control like that. That she didn't trust men, except Ted, of course, was her own private demon, which she normally kept well hidden. And for it to have come out so venomously shocked her. The frown on her face deepened. She didn't like admitting it, in fact she hated admitting it, but Frank Davidson unnerved her. She didn't know why. Normally she was totally immune to men. But her body, at least, seemed to be acutely aware of his touch. I'm just worried about Ted and that has me rattled, she reasoned.

Determinedly shoving the parking lot exchange to the back of her mind, she tried to come up with a new plan. She considered the idea of a private detective but she had no idea how to find a good one and then there was the cost to consider. The lawyer wasn't cheap and even though Ted was covered by insurance, she guessed there would still be extra hospital and doctor bills.

She was driving by Frank's place on her way to Ted's apartment when an idea struck her. Turning the car around, she drove back and turned down the road marked "Davidson's Trucking." The gate of the high wire fence surrounding the property was closed and locked. As she parked in front of it and climbed out of the car, two large German shepherds came running toward her barking ferociously. Grateful the fence was between them and her, she sat down on the hood of Ted's car and waited. Fairly quickly, the dogs grew tired of barking and sat and watched her. To the left of the garage-office complex she noticed a brick walkway leading to a well-kept two-story frame house set in a small clearing surrounded by large old trees. She'd been so tired and upset when she'd been here yesterday that she'd barely noticed the house then, but now she remembered that Ted had said Frank lived next to the garage. She found herself wondering what it looked like inside, then scowled. How Frank Davidson lived was of no interest to her!

Turning her attention to the large gravel parking area in front of the garage, she drew a breath of relief when she saw four trucks parked there. She knew Frank had had nine to begin with but not only had the merchandise been stolen from five of them, the trucks had been taken, too. He'd have to come back here before he could start his latest run.

She'd been there about twenty minutes when he drove up in his pickup and came to a stop beside her. He switched off his engine and climbed out. Approaching her, he said impatiently, "I don't have any time for another argument. I've got a job to do. So state your business and be brief."

Sliding off the hood of the car, her chin was set in a determined line as she faced him. "I'm going with you on this run."

For a moment he stared at her in disbelief, then his jaw hardened. "No, you're not. Now that that's settled, I'll open the gate, you drive in, turn around and get out of here."

Laura's shoulders stiffened. "I'm coming. If you won't let me ride with you, then I'll follow in Ted's car. Catching the real crooks is the only way to help my brother."

Frank's gaze narrowed dangerously. "You'd be a lot more help to him if you'd leave me alone."

Laura dug her heels in. "Look, I don't like your company any better than you like mine, but we both want the same thing. We both want the real crooks caught."

The scowl on his face deepened. "This run could be dangerous," he said tersely. "I don't want to have to worry about you."

"You don't have to worry about me," she assured him. "And I'm coming one way or another."

For a long moment he stared at her indecisively, then said grudgingly, "All right, you can ride along."

Laura smiled triumphantly. "I knew we could come to a reasonable agreement," she said brightly.

Frank shook his head as if to say he wasn't certain which of them was the craziest. "But you stay out of the way if there's trouble," he ordered.

"Of course," she said, hardly able to believe she had actually talked herself into this chance to help Ted.

The expression on Frank's face suggested he didn't believe this assurance for one second and he hesitated again, then, with a shrug of his shoulders as if to say he realized he didn't have any choice, he unlocked the gate.

When it swung open, Laura froze as the two dogs ran toward her barking loudly.

"Stand!" Frank ordered and the dogs came to an abrupt halt. "They make a lot of noise but they won't bite," he assured her.

Laura wasn't convinced and she continued to watch the German shepherds dubiously.

"Stop baring your fangs. She's a friend," Frank said and the dogs moved toward her, their tails wagging happily.

"Do they have names?" she asked, petting them tentatively. They were large, and she was still remembering how ferociously they had run at her when she'd first driven up.

"Rough and Ready," he replied a little sheepishly.

"Cute," she muttered, with a crooked grin.

For one brief moment there was a soft answering smile in Frank's eyes, and Laura experienced a curious warm curling in her abdomen. Then his manner suddenly became coolly businesslike once again. "Enough socializing," he said. "Home!" The two dogs took off in the direction of the garage. Climbing back into his pickup, he glanced toward Laura. "If you're coming, let's get going."

A few minutes later she was seated in the cab of the eighteen wheeler and Frank was guiding the semi out onto the main road. It was a big cab, with captain's chairs for the driver and passenger and a bunk in the rear. The more distance between us the better, she thought, glancing toward the man behind the wheel. Although she and Frank were practically sworn enemies, he'd insisted on helping her up into her seat, and again his touch had sent currents of heat shooting through her. Then there had been her reaction to the brief moment of warmth she'd seen in his eyes. Considering her long-practiced immunity to men, the effect he was having on her was decidedly unnerving. Glancing back, she saw the two dogs standing by the fence. "I didn't see your pets yesterday," she said, determinedly turning her thoughts away from the disturbing reactions she was having to this trucker.

"They have a pen with a large run behind the garage. I keep them in there when I have the place open to the public," he answered with cool politeness. "Wouldn't want to scare off any customers."

Deciding the dogs were a safe subject, she persisted. "Who feeds them while you're gone?"

"Maryann Johnson." Anger returned to his voice. "Had to lay off my full time secretary and go back to running the office on a shoestring with an answering machine and part-time help. Lucky for me, Maryann prefers temporary work and can come in on a moment's notice. She'll take care of the office and the dogs while I'm gone. And she has her own set of keys so we don't have to wait around for her to get here."

A vision of a tall, slinky blond in skin-tight jeans filled Laura's mind, and she wondered what Maryann Johnson did for Frank when he was in town. The thought caused an uncomfortable twinge in the pit of her stomach. Scowling at herself, she sat back and tried to think of some other topic of conversation to pass the time. None came to mind. Glancing toward her companion she saw the hard set of his jaw, reminding her that he was not happy about having her along. It's going to be a long ride, she decided and settled for watching the scenery.

Pulling over on the side of the road in front of the farmhouse where Ted's apartment was, Frank set the truck in gear. "We're going to Denver. You might want to pack a few things. But make it fast."

"If you try to leave without me, I'll follow," she warned.

He rewarded this threat with a scowl. "Just be quick and don't pack your whole wardrobe."

Laura jogged across the lawn and took the stairs two at a time. Grabbing only what she considered essential, she was packed and back at the truck within ten minutes.

Frank seemed a little surprised that she'd followed his instructions so well, but he didn't say anything. After he shoved her bag into the storage compartment at the rear of the cab, they again started down the road.

Twenty minutes later, he still hadn't said anything to her and she was beginning to wonder if they were going to make the entire run to Denver and back in silence. Suddenly without looking at her, he ordered, "Climb into the bunk and zip the flap closed."

Startled by this command, she frowned. "I realize you aren't thrilled with my company, but don't you think sequestering me in the bunk is going a little too far?"

The hint of a smile played at the corners of his mouth, then his expression again became serious. "Hayes is nervous enough about my carrying his stuff," he explained with gruff impatience. "It'll be best if he doesn't know I have a passenger, especially a female."

Nodding her understanding, she unfastened her seat belt and, slipping between the captain's chairs, she climbed onto the bunk. Sitting with her legs crossed in Indian fashion, she unrolled the heavy canvas flap that served to enclose the bunk for privacy and zipped it closed. Secluded in her dark cocoon, she noticed the faint trace of Frank's after-shave. It taunted her senses, and a curiously warm little knot threatened to form in her abdomen. *Stop behaving so ridiculously,* she chided herself. She'd been resistant to men since her father's funeral. Not only that, she and Frank Davidson had been at one another's throats ever since they met. She couldn't possibly be attracted to him! *I'm just overwrought with worry about Ted,* she reasoned and ignored the disquieting sensations Frank aroused in her.

The truck made a sharp turn and she almost fell. Deciding it was safer to lie down, she stretched out on the bunk and braced herself as Frank made another turn. Then she felt the truck backing up. We must be getting into position at the loading dock, she decided and gave herself a mental pat on the back when she heard the truck being opened and boxes or crates being loaded inside.

It seemed like forever, but finally she heard the back being closed. A couple of minutes later, Frank climbed into the cab. He waited until they were again on the main road before telling her she could come out.

Slipping back into the passenger seat, she glanced toward him. As her gaze rested on the line of his jaw, she wondered what it would feel like to run her finger along it. Shocked, she jerked her gaze away. Again assuring herself that she was just tense and overreacting to everything and everyone around her, she concentrated on the scenery.

Frank turned onto the Pennsylvania Turnpike heading west. They'd been traveling for nearly three-quarters of an hour when he again broke the silence in the cab. "There is one thing I'm curious about," he said.

The edge of cynicism in his voice caused her guard to come up. "What is it?"

"I was wondering who you really are?"

She frowned at him in confusion. "You know who I am. I'm Ted's sister."

He shook his head. "That's not what I mean. What I want to know is if you're the straightlaced, conservative woman who confronted me yesterday or the flirtatious cowgirl I saw in the Twenty-Four Hours Café."

She glared at him. "I am not a flirtatious cowgirl! I told you I was trying to help my brother."

He raised a skeptical eyebrow. "By flirting with Joe Monroe?"

He's arrogant, bullheaded and judgmental, she noted coldly, increasing her list of descriptive adjectives. Regarding him with dignified poise, she said, "I don't have to answer to you for any of my actions."

"No, you don't," he agreed. Again his mouth formed a hard straight line signaling an end to the conversation. Picking up a cassette lying on the dash, he shoved it into the player beneath the radio and as the silence again descended between them, the sound of country music filled the cab.

A couple of hours down the road, they pulled into one of the turnpike rest stops.

"You've got ten minutes," he told her, as he set the brake and turned off the engine. "Then we're out of here. I got a late start."

As he reached for his door handle, she frowned. "Shouldn't we take turns staying with the truck?"

"I'll lock it," he replied.

"Locking them hasn't been too successful in the past," she pointed out tersely, wondering how he could be so worried about his trucks one minute and so cavalier about them the next.

His gaze narrowed. "Look, you invited yourself along on this ride. We do things my way with no questions asked or you go home."

She added "bossy" to the list of adjectives she was compiling to describe him as she climbed out of the cab.

After using the facilities, she wandered over to the assortment of candy near the cash register. Whenever she got upset she always developed a strong craving for chocolate. And right now that craving was monumental. Picking up several chocolate bars, she paid for them. Then spotting the bank of phones nearby, she hurried toward it. She'd promised to go by the hospital and visit with Ted. He'd worry when she didn't show up. She also guessed he would be very unhappy with her when he found out what she was up to. Briefly she considered lying to him, but there had never been lies between them before and now was not the time to start, she decided as she dialed the number.

"I can't believe you're doing this," he said anxiously when she told him where she was. "It could be dangerous."

"It's the only way I've been able to come up with to help you," she pointed out matter-of-factly, then with a confidence she didn't really feel, she added, "I know how to take care of myself."

"I don't want you hurt because of me," Ted insisted curtly. "I want you to give this up and return here immediately."

Feeling a prickling sensation at the nape of her neck, Laura glanced over her shoulder to discover Frank watching her from near the doors. "Got to run," she replied. "See you in a few days." Before he could make any further protests, she hung up.

"Who were you talking to?" Frank asked as he guided the truck onto the turnpike a few minutes later. In spite of his attempt to sound nonchalant, Laura heard suspicion in his voice.

"I called Ted so he wouldn't worry when I didn't show up at the hospital," she replied.

He glanced toward her, his expression unreadable. "Did you tell him what you were up to?"

"I told him I was making a run with you," she replied, opening her bag and taking out one of the chocolate bars.

"What'd he say?"

"He didn't like me being here any more than you like me being here. He wanted me to come back immediately," she answered.

Frank had been watching the road. Now he glanced toward her and she saw that the suspicion in his eyes had deepened. "He did, did he?" he muttered as he again concentrated on the road.

Fervently Laura wished she'd made Ted's demand sound less emphatic. It was clear that Frank was taking her brother's concern the wrong way. Obviously he was thinking that Ted knew there was going to be a robbery and didn't want her involved. "He's always been overly protective of me," she elaborated quickly. "He doesn't think I should get mixed up in this."

"He's right," Frank agreed grimly.

Ordering herself to think before she spoke in the future, she took a bite of the candy.

Glancing toward her, Frank frowned. "Sorry," he apologized curtly. "If I'd known you were hungry, I'd have given you time to get something decent to eat. There are some ham sandwiches and fruit in the cooler behind your seat. You're welcome to whatever you want."

"Thanks, but I'm not hungry," she replied.

Keeping his eyes on the road, he raised a skeptical eyebrow.

"I get cravings for chocolate when I'm nervous or worried," she explained self-consciously. Again the slight aroma of his after-shave teased her senses and she heard herself adding, "It's the only craving I allow myself to indulge in."

He glanced toward her. Momentarily, there was a glimmer of heat in the dark depths of his eyes. Then it vanished. "It's always a good idea to be cautious where cravings are concerned," he agreed evenly.

For a moment Laura found herself wondering if he was fighting against an unwanted attraction to her, the same way she was fighting one that drew her to him. Then she frowned at herself. That was crazy! He considered her a nuisance. Besides, even if he were interested in her, she certainly wasn't going to allow herself to become interested in him! She took another bite.

"Eating chocolate in the middle of the morning." He shook his head and grinned. "Never knew a true chocoholic before."

It was the first time she'd seen him really smile. It gave gentler lines to his face and she found herself feeling disconcerted by how truly warm those dark eyes of his could look when they weren't filled with anger. Then as if he were angry with himself for letting down his guard and actually being friendly with the enemy, his jaw tensed and the smile vanished. His grim manner returned and he again gave his full attention to the road.

I prefer the frown, anyway. It's safer, she decided, still feeling slightly shaken by the side of Frank Davidson she'd just witnessed. Attempting to put Frank out of her mind, she took another bite of the candy. But the chocolate had suddenly lost its appeal and, rewrapping the bar, she shoved it into the bag with the others.

Around two o'clock they stopped for a late lunch. While she was finishing her coffee, Frank left to fill his truck with gas and check the oil and water.

Later as they pulled onto the turnpike, he said, "We'll be making a sleeping stop around ten. I called ahead and booked a room. Don't want my log to get too off base."

The words *a room* echoed in Laura's mind and her back stiffened. Over the past year and a half, Ted had talked a great deal about Frank. He'd said that Frank was the true cavalier type, always ready to help a lady in distress and never expecting any favors in return. My brother always was a bit on the naive side, she mused cynically. Not only was Frank Davidson no knight in shining armor, he wasn't even subtle about his demands. Well, if he thought she was going to sleep with him just to try to change his mind about her brother, he'd better think again. "I'll sleep in the truck," she said coolly.

He tossed her an impatient glance. "I'll be sleeping in the truck." His gaze narrowed as if he'd suddenly read her mind and he added dryly, "You don't have to worry about me. The only thing in that motel room I've got the least bit of interest in is the shower, and I plan to use that solo."

Laura felt her cheeks redden. She knew she should be pleased with this assurance but instead she felt insulted. I am so worried about Ted, I'm in serious danger of totally losing my perspective on life, she chided herself.

Determined not to let her mind dwell on her disquieting companion, she concentrated on the traffic around and behind them. Ahead of them was a station wagon with a man, a woman and three kids. She'd seen the vehicle when it first entered the turnpike that morning. The license plate was from Missouri, and she guessed the occupants were on their way home from a vacation. A red sports car whipped past them and she recognized it as another car she'd spotted when they first entered the turnpike. Clearly the driver must have stopped longer for lunch than he intended and now he was speeding to make up for lost time. Not smart, she noted. In the large rearview mirror on her side, she saw a green coupe. It had been with them since around their first stop. There was a single male inside.

Looking ahead, she saw the flashing lights of a police car. The driver of the red sports car was getting a ticket.

"It's amazing how the traffic is all traveling at different rates and pulling off at different places and yet there are several cars we're constantly passing or having pass us," she said musingly, recognizing yet another vehicle, a blue van with two men inside.

"There does seem to be a certain rhythm to it," Frank replied.

But in spite of his effort to appear disinterested, she caught the subtle edge in his voice and knew he was watching the traffic carefully. She called herself thickheaded as it dawned on her that the robbers would have to follow Frank's truck because they would not know what route he would take. She, too, began to watch the vehicles around them with greater interest.

Early evening they left the turnpike, turning west onto Interstate 70. The station wagon, blue van, red sports car, which was now staying within a reasonable range of the speed limit, and the green coupe all turned off with them. The station wagon, however, left the interstate fairly soon afterward. Going to get a good night's rest before they start again tomorrow, Laura decided.

Periodically, over the next four hours, one or the other of the remaining three vehicles would turn off but would always turn up again after a while.

They were better than halfway through Ohio when Frank finally pulled off for the night. She noticed that the sports car kept going but both the green coupe and blue van took the same turnoff. Neither, however, pulled in at the motel Frank had chosen.

Glancing toward him, Laura felt a surge of relief that this day was over. They'd barely spoken, and the silence between them had her nerves on a brittle edge. She frowned down at the practically untouched bag of chocolate bars. I've never known a man who could kill my craving for chocolate, she mused. Then assuring herself that it was the situation she found herself in and not Frank Davidson that was truly disturbing her, she climbed out of the cab.

Chapter Three

It was a little after ten when Laura entered her motel room and sank down into a chair. The room wasn't plush, but it was clean and comfortable. Even more important, it was private.

She stretched, then gave her body a shake as if trying to get rid of the tension that had gripped her while sharing the cab of the truck with Frank. It didn't work. Even with the wall and several feet of pavement between them, she still felt his presence. Pulling the curtain open a crack, she looked out. His truck was parked where she had a full view of the side of it.

While she watched, Frank came around the truck carrying her bag and a leather satchel. As he walked toward her room, her muscles stiffened painfully. "He's just a man," she chided herself curtly. Still, she couldn't rid herself of the uneasiness she felt as she released the curtain and opened the door. She told herself to ignore his presence but the room suddenly seemed ten times smaller. She had to get out. Besides, she reasoned, refusing to admit she was running scared from a man, it was the proper thing to do.

"I'll be back in around half an hour or forty-five minutes," she said, grabbing her purse and the room key as he entered and set his satchel on the table. "I'm going to the restaurant for a cup of coffee."

She barely noticed his nod that he'd heard her as she swiftly exited the room, closing the door behind her.

Outside she took a couple of deep breaths. You're behaving like a foolish schoolgirl who's never been around a man in her life, she scolded herself. Besides, to have any reaction to Frank Davidson was totally ridiculous. Although she did have sympathy for his position, he *was* trying to put her brother into prison. Not only that, he was arrogant, self-righteous, bullheaded and bossy. "I don't even like him," she muttered under her breath. Then her traitorous mind suddenly remembered his smile.

He's probably charmed a million women with that look, she berated herself. Determinedly pushing him out of her mind, she glanced at the parking lot as she walked toward the restaurant. Suddenly she came to an abrupt halt. Her eyes narrowed as she looked harder. The blue van was there, parked in a far corner. Practically holding her breath, she scanned the rest of the parking lot. On the other side, closer to Frank's truck, she saw the green coupe.

Trying not to be obvious in case anyone was watching, she turned and forced herself to walk at a reasonably sedate pace back to the room. Entering, she froze. Frank had removed his boots and was just tossing his shirt onto a chair. As her eyes rested on the broad expanse of his dark-haired chest, a hot, curling sensation began in her abdomen and threatened to spread through her. Stop it! she ordered herself frantically.

"You're back a little soon," he said, studying her coldly. "And I would have thought you would at least have had the courtesy to knock." Then abruptly his eyes raked her as a cynical smile suddenly curled his lips. "Or have you decided to try another ploy in an attempt to help your brother?"

Laura flushed scarlet at the implication in his voice. "If you're suggesting I came back to try to seduce you," she said through clenched teeth, "you're mistaken. It'll be a cold day in hell before I would want you in my bed."

She caught a flicker of dry amusement in the dark depths of his eyes before they became shuttered. "Then, why *are* you back?" he questioned.

"I saw the blue van and the green coupe in the parking lot. Both of them acted as if they were going someplace else, but they're here," she replied stiffly.

He gave a nonchalant shrug of his shoulders. "They probably couldn't find a room anywhere else."

She scowled at him. "Don't you think you should at least consider the possibility that one or both of those vehicles might be driven by the bad guys?"

His nonchalance was replaced by impatient anger. "I'm considering all kinds of possibilities. In the meantime, I don't want you running around upsetting everything with hysterical accusations."

She glared at him. "Hysterical accusations! I'm trying to save my brother and catch the real crooks by making a few very astute observations and you call them hysterical accusations?"

He drew a breath. "If you really want to help, you'll go have that cup of coffee, don't talk to anyone, don't do anything. Just drink your coffee in peace and quiet and let me do the worrying."

Suddenly as if a light bulb had just flashed on in her head, the truth dawned on her. Calling herself thickheaded for a second time today, she studied him narrowly. "This is all a setup, isn't it? You're using that truck as bait to catch the crooks."

He raked a hand through his hair in an agitated manner. "Just go have your coffee and let me take my shower."

"Fine, I'll go," she growled.

But as her hand reached for the doorknob, he suddenly crossed the room in four long strides and caught her wrist. "And don't do *anything*," he ordered, scowling down at her darkly. "Not *anything*. Just drink your coffee and mind your own business."

His touch felt like fire against her skin, and she had the most incredible urge to reach out with her free hand and test the feel of the crisp, curly hairs on his chest. Shocked by this wanton reaction, she jerked free. "You don't have to worry about me. All I want is for the real crooks to be caught," she assured him tightly, again reaching for the knob. This time he didn't stop her.

Outside, she angrily noticed that her hands were shaking. He evoked urges in her she had trained herself never to have. It's the situation, not the man, she told herself again. I'm just overwrought. When this is all over and Ted is safe from being thrown in jail, I won't even notice Frank Davidson is around.

Reaching the restaurant, she chose a booth and ordered a cup of coffee. The windows of the place faced in the wrong direction and she couldn't see the part of the parking lot where Frank's truck was parked or where the blue van and the green coupe were located. She considered the possibility of taking her coffee and standing outside where she could see them but she'd promised Frank she would do nothing. If he had a trap set, she certainly didn't want to ruin it.

Too tense to just sit, she glanced at her watch. It was nearly eleven-thirty. But that was Pennsylvania time. It was only ten-thirty Kansas City time. She could call Peg Norman and find out what was happening at work. She and Peg had been friends for years, and Laura knew Peg wouldn't mind a late call. "I just need to hear a friendly voice," she muttered as she dialed.

She was feeling somewhat better, more like her old self when she hung up a few minutes later. But the feeling evaporated when she turned and discovered Frank watching her.

"That was certainly a quick shower," she said as he joined her.

Ignoring the remark, his gaze traveled to the phone and then to her. "Isn't it a little late to be calling Ted?"

She saw the suspicion in his eyes and her back stiffened. "I was calling a friend in Kansas City."

"Well, he's not a very good friend if he let you come out here by yourself and get mixed up in this mess," he observed dryly.

She regarded him coolly. "It wasn't a he, it was a she and nobody tells me what I can do and can't do."

The frown on Frank's face deepened. "Well, if you're going to keep traveling with me, I'm telling you to go back to your room and go to bed."

Laura was tempted to inform him that she'd go back to her room when she pleased but the look on his face warned her he meant business. "I was only waiting for you to get finished with your shower," she replied, and without a backward glance, she left the restaurant and returned to her room.

Stripping out of her clothes, she again remembered the suspicion she'd seen in Frank's eyes when he glanced toward the phone, then to her. If this trap doesn't work, he'll probably think I warned the real crooks, she realized. Then he'll feel certain I'm one of them, too, if he doesn't already. "You've really gotten yourself in a fine mess," she informed the pale image staring out at her from the mirror. "Frank's plan had better work."

Wishing she hadn't given in to the impulse to call Peg, she dropped her undergarments in the sink to soak, then climbed into the shower.

Trying not to think of the web she was weaving around herself, she was rinsing the lather from her hair when she thought she heard a movement in her room. Thinking Frank must have forgotten something, she peeked around the curtain. The smell of gasoline suddenly assailed her nostrils and she saw a large, hairy arm reach into the bathroom and grab the door. It definitely wasn't Frank's arm. As the door was slammed shut, she caught the flash of a piece of metal being inserted between the door and the jamb. For a long moment she stood frozen with fear. Then, grabbing a towel, she wrapped it around her torso as she stepped out of the tub. Cautiously she tried the door. It wouldn't open. She turned the knob and pulled harder. It was jammed tightly shut. Maybe that's just as well, she thought, still hearing noises in her room. If she couldn't get out, no one could get in, either. Suddenly there was a sound like a huge puff, followed by a door opening and closing. Whoever had been there was gone.

She was about to breath a sigh of relief when she smelled the smoke. Whoever had locked her in the bathroom had set fire to her room. Terror filled her.

"Help!" she screamed, pounding on the door and hoping the walls of the motel were thin enough to allow a guest in a nearby room to hear her.

The smoke alarm in the bedroom began to ring shrilly. Tears caused by the smoke coming in under the door mingled with her tears of fear. "Help!" she screamed again. Another cry was strangled by a fit of coughing.

"Laura?"

It was Frank's voice calling out to her.

"I'm in here!" she yelled back, again pounding on the bathroom door. "Someone jammed the door closed. I can't get it open."

"Stand back," he ordered. "I'm going to have to kick it open."

Clutching the towel that was threatening to fall, she stepped into the tub. She heard his boot hit the wood at about the level of the knob but the door remained solidly closed. Frank kicked again. On the third try, the door flew open.

Billowing clouds of smoke filled the air. Before she could move, Frank was picking her up and carrying her outside.

As they passed the smoldering bed, she saw a man with a fire extinguisher putting out the burning mattress. Still in a state of panic, she wasn't thinking above an emotional level, and on that level she found a feeling of safety in Frank's arms. Tears of terror continued to stream down her cheeks. Holding on to him even tighter, she buried her face in his neck.

"You're going to be all right," he assured her gruffly as they stepped out into the cool night air.

He felt so strong and comforting. Coughing violently, Laura clung to him even tighter.

When the firemen arrived and took over the job of putting out the fire, the man who had been using the fire extinguisher joined Frank. "Is she all right?" he asked brusquely.

"Just scared," Frank answered in the same brusque tone.

"Smelled like they used gasoline," the other man said.

"You can take her in here," a third man directed, opening the door of a room a couple of doors away. Peeking over Frank's shoulder, Laura saw that the third man had a ring of keys and decided he had to be the manager or owner. Beyond him she saw clusters of people in robes and slippers being encouraged to return to their rooms. "Probably a smoking accident," she heard one man say as the firemen carried out the smoldering mattress. Turning to the woman beside him, he added pointedly, "That should be a lesson to you."

Laura missed the woman's response. Frank carried her into the room, and her nerves had become settled enough for her to realize she was clinging to him as if her life depended on it. Flushing with embarrassment, she lifted her head off his shoulder and unwrapped her arms from their death grip around his neck. The flush turned scarlet when she realized she was only loosely wrapped in a towel.

"I'll call a doctor," the manager said. Before Laura could protest, he was gone.

"Pull back the covers, Jim," Frank ordered the man who had been using the fire extinguisher. As soon as Jim obeyed, Frank laid her on the bed and tossed the covers over her.

Laura's hands were shaking as she clutched the blankets around her chin. She'd felt the tenseness in Frank's body and seen the relief in his eyes when he'd finally been able to get rid of her. He hated holding me, she thought, and her embarrassment multiplied. But when she blinked the smoke and tears out of her eyes and looked up into his face, her chin trembled. There was a look of concern in his eyes that sent a surge of warmth coursing through her.

"How do you feel?" the man named Jim asked her.

"Shaken," she answered, still lost in the dark comforting depths of Frank's eyes. Then, as if he were angry with himself for showing kindness to the enemy, Frank's gaze again became cold and calculating. Defensively, Laura's chin tightened and she shifted her attention to Jim. He was about Frank's height and age. His hair was a dark blond, his eyes blue and his features more gently cut than Frank's, giving him a boyishly handsome appearance.

"The most important question," Frank interjected grimly, "is why does someone want to kill you?"

In spite of the warm coverings, Laura shivered as she remembered being trapped in the bathroom. "I don't know."

"I do," Jim said with an angry growl as he glanced out the window toward the parking lot. "It was a diversion. The truck's gone. They used the fire to lure us both away from it at the same time."

Suspicion etched itself deep into Frank's features, and Laura's chin tightened even more. "I had nothing to do with your missing truck," she said tightly.

Ignoring her protest, Jim scowled at Frank. "I don't understand why you brought her along in the first place."

"She threatened to follow me if I didn't," Frank replied curtly. "We would've looked like a caravan. I thought it would be less conspicuous if she rode with me."

Shaking his head, Jim headed toward the door. "I'll notify the police and see if I can find the truck." Glancing at Frank, he added pointedly, "You stay here and take care of the little lady."

"I'll help find the truck," Frank said, heading for the door ahead of Jim.

"I'm the investigator. I've got the equipment and the connections with the police," Jim pointed out in a reasoning tone. "You just make certain Miss Martin doesn't leave. We may want to question her."

Scowling, Frank grudgingly stepped aside while Laura groaned mentally. Obviously this Jim person was some sort of detective Frank was working with to catch the thieves. Equally obvious, he suspected her of being in cahoots with the crooks, too.

Jim's departure was followed almost immediately by the arrival of a policeman to take Laura's and Frank's statements about the fire. Sitting in the bed with the covers wrapped securely around her, Laura's nerves were on a brittle edge. She'd never felt so vulnerable or so frightened. Just stay calm, she ordered herself. The years of holding a tight rein over her emotions paid off and she was able to keep her voice level.

"So you think the fire was simply a diversion to cover the theft of your truck?" the policeman asked when he finished gathering all the information.

"Looks that way," Frank replied. "Jim Halsey, an investigator with my insurance company, is reporting the theft right now. We only realized it had happened just before you came in."

"Sounds like you're dealing with some real dangerous types," the policeman commented. "You better take care of yourselves."

"We will," Frank assured him, but the angry look he cast in Laura's direction let her know that he didn't think of the two of them as being on the same side.

A protest formed on Laura's tongue but she ordered herself to keep quiet. She didn't need the policeman discovering that Frank was suspicious of her. But the moment the door closed behind the lawman and she and Frank were alone in the room, her control snapped. "You think I'm involved with the crooks, don't you?" she demanded curtly.

"I don't want to believe it," he replied, standing with his thumbs hooked through the belt loops on his jeans while he studied her grimly. "But you were making a very late call."

"I told you who I called," she replied tersely. "Peg and I have been friends for years. I know she doesn't go to bed before eleven. And I needed to hear a friendly voice."

"Let's say I believe you. That still leaves another possibility," he continued in the same grim tone.

"And what is that?" she asked tiredly, knowing she wasn't going to like what he was about to say but needing to hear it, anyway.

"The crooks could have devised a simpler diversion, one that wouldn't have left them facing a possible murder charge, so I have to ask myself why they chose to set fire to your room," he elaborated. "The answer I came up with is that maybe they were trying to kill two birds with one stone. Maybe they were afraid Ted might have told you something you shouldn't know so they decided to get rid of you at the same time they heisted the truck."

"Ted didn't tell me anything because he doesn't *know* anything," she insisted angrily. Glaring at him, she added, "You are the most bullheaded man I've ever met."

A smile tilted one corner of his mouth. "My mother and sisters have accused me of that, too."

Again she saw a gentleness in his eyes that shook her, then his expression hardened once again.

He really doesn't trust me, she mused, wondering if he was picturing her in the cell next to Ted. She was about to protest her innocence again when a knock on the door interrupted her.

It was the doctor. After sending Frank outside, he made a thorough examination of Laura and declared her fit.

Frank reentered as the doctor left. He was carrying her overnight bag and her clothes. Dropping her shoes, jeans and sweater on a chair, he placed her suitcase on the bed, then carried her panties and bra to the sink and began washing them out.

A flush of embarrassment spread upward from her neck. "You don't have to do that."

"Don't want them cluttering up the sink all night," he replied matter of factly, quickly rinsing them and tossing them over a hanger.

Watching him, Laura felt as if she had lost control of everything around her. I need to get dressed, she decided, but as she began pulling out clothes, Frank's shoulders straightened.

"A nightgown should suffice," he said, watching her in the mirror. It was an order, not a suggestion.

She glared at him. "I'll put on what I please."

"You'll put on a nightgown and get some sleep," he ordered, "or I'll dress you myself."

It was clear he meant it. Tossing him a scowl, she shoved the clothes back into the case and pulled out a cotton nightgown. Keeping herself discreetly concealed with the covers, she worked herself into it. "You don't have to stand guard over me all night," she said, unnerved by his continued presence. "I give you my word I'm not going anywhere."

"I've got no place to go," he replied, adding pointedly, "my bed got stolen." Switching on the television set, he lay down on the other bed. "Besides, I promised both Jim and the policeman I'd keep an eye on you."

She glanced over at him, determined to insist that he leave. But that would be like trying to move a mountain, she decided as her gaze traveled along his long form. Besides, although she hated admitting it, she did still feel badly shaken. And, while Frank might want her in jail, he wouldn't try to murder her. Giving in to the need for the security she felt in his presence, she kept quiet. But only because I'm still recovering from a bad scare, she assured herself. By morning, she'd have her control back in place and she wouldn't be needing any man's presence to give her a feeling of safety.

Attempting to ignore him, she found her hair dryer and finished drying her still damp hair. But Frank was not an easy man to ignore. Against her will, she found herself glancing toward him covertly several times. He, on the other hand, obviously found her very easy to ignore. His total attention remained focused on the baseball game being televised.

There was no doubt in her mind that she was also perfectly safe from any advances by him. This thought should have been comforting, but it wasn't. Furious with the ambiguity of her muddled emotions, she lay down and pulled the covers up around her chin. Though she felt exhausted, she was certain she would never actually be able to sleep with him in the room. But exhaustion won and within minutes she was asleep.

But sleep did not provide an escape. In nightmare form, she relived the fire. Her heart pounded wildly in fear and she tossed and struggled and cried out for help. Tears trickled down her cheeks.

"You're safe, Laura." Frank's gruff voice penetrated her consciousness.

Vaguely, still half asleep, she was aware of him bending over her. His thumb brushed a trail of tears from her cheek. Reaching up, her hands closed around the fabric of his shirt like the hands of a drowning man around a life preserver. "Help me," she heard a female voice saying and realized it was her own.

"I won't let anyone harm you," he promised gruffly.

The bed shifted as he lay down beside her.

Still clutching his shirt, she snuggled into his arms.

"Go back to sleep now," he ordered, and she did.

Chapter Four

Laura awoke the next morning to the sound of light snoring near her ear. Opening her eyes a crack, she saw her hands still holding on to Frank's shirt. She'd thought the whole thing had been a dream. Obviously it hadn't been. An embarrassed flush spread over her. But even more distressing than the embarrassment was the excitement lying in his arms stirred within her. I really don't need this kind of complication in my life, she chided herself.

Releasing her hold on him, she started to move quietly out of his arms. The snoring stopped. Looking up she met his dark gaze. For a brief moment, she again saw a warmth in his eyes that caused her heart to pound erratically, then it was replaced by suspicion. And with the suspicion, she saw a question. He was again wondering if she was trying to seduce him in an effort to win him over to her side.

To her chagrin, she actually found herself wondering what it would feel like to kiss him. She avoided looking directly at him as she scooted out of the bed, grabbed her clothes and went into the bathroom to dress.

While he shaved, she brushed her hair, then plaited it into a French pigtail that hung down the center of her back. Watching herself and him in the mirror, she found herself thinking that lovers must have played out this same scene in this same room millions of times. Here she was sitting on the bed doing her hair while he stood, shoeless and shirtless, in front of the sink shaving. But instead of the intimacy there would have been between lovers, there was a tension in the room that could have been cut with a knife.

"Thanks for seeing me through my nightmares," she said, finally finding the courage to mention spending the night in his arms.

"No problem," he replied dryly. "Couldn't get any sleep with you tossing and turning like that, anyway."

Clearly she could have been an inanimate object as far as he was concerned, she thought. Well, that was the way she wanted it.

He was still shaving when she finished with her hair. In spite of all of her self-chiding, the sight of the broad expanse of his muscular back was continuing to have a decidedly unnerving effect on her. Think inanimate object, she ordered herself. But it didn't work. Aloud she said, "I'm going to get some breakfast."

His face still partly covered with shaving cream, he blocked her path. "You'll wait for me."

She started to argue, then held her tongue. She didn't need to do anything else that would make her look more suspicious in his eyes. "I'll wait," she conceded and reseated herself on the bed.

An hour later, they were in the restaurant finishing breakfast when Jim joined them.

"Been up all night, but it was worth it," he said with a Cheshire grin as he seated himself and ordered a cup of coffee. "The homing device worked like a charm. We caught the bad guys and found all your missing trucks. They've been repainted but other than that, they're in good condition."

"Homing device?" Laura questioned sharply. She started to demand to know why they hadn't mentioned this to her. She'd been certain the crooks had gotten away scot-free. Then she stopped herself. She knew the answer. They thought she might try to warn the robbers.

"We wanted to find out how they were getting away with the trucks so quickly and where they were taking them," Jim elaborated. He shook his head in awe. "It was a great setup. They had these magnetic signs they fitted over Frank's logo and they changed the license plate. The police would have passed them right up if we hadn't had the bug planted in the cab."

Grimly Frank glanced toward Laura, then back to Jim. "What about Ted?" he questioned.

"He's clean," Jim replied, giving Laura a smile, then turning his attention to Frank. "One of the guys we picked up confessed Ted was set up to be the patsy to shift suspicion away from the real culprit. He also told us that the robberies of the other trucking companies were just to spread the suspicion around, too. Miss Martin was right. You were the real target. Their boss was Bill Kyle."

Laura breathed a sigh of relief. "Thank goodness."

"Bill Kyle." Frank frowned darkly. "I thought he was in jail."

Jim shook his head in a gesture of disbelief. "Got out on early parole... would you believe for good behavior?"

"Who's Bill Kyle?" Laura questioned, wanting to know about the man who had almost caused her brother to be sent to jail and her to an early grave.

"He was a driver who used to work for me," Frank answered. "I found out he was transporting drugs as well as the goods he was supposed to be carrying. I helped the police catch him."

"When he got out, he was bent on revenge." Jim picked up the story. "His plan was to run Frank out of business, while at the same time setting himself up with a trucking line using Frank's trucks."

"So that wraps it up," Frank said with a note of finality. "I'm back in business."

"You're back in business," Jim confirmed. "But it's not quite wrapped up yet. We haven't picked up Kyle. He wounded a policeman and got out the back while we were rounding up all the others." Jim smiled reassuringly. "But don't worry. We've got an all states' bulletin out on him. He'll be picked up soon." Yawning, he added, "I just need you to sign these papers for the police." He shoved a handful of documents in front of Frank.

After reading through them quickly, Frank signed them.

Jim yawned again as he put the papers in his pocket. "I'll arrange for you to get your trucks back as soon as possible. Now I'm going to get some well-deserved sleep."

"I'm glad Ted was cleared," Frank said when he and Laura were alone. With gruff self-consciousness, he added, "I know you probably won't believe it, but I do like him and I didn't like thinking he was one of the bad guys."

"Thanks," she replied. There was honest remorse in his voice. "The evidence against him was pretty strong," she admitted.

A crooked smile of relief played at one corner of Frank's mouth. "I'm going to rent a car and drive back to Chadds Ford as soon as we finish breakfast. I've got a business I've got to rebuild. You're welcome to ride along. I figure you want to get back to Ted as soon as possible." As he met her gaze levelly, the crooked smile vanished and regret filled his voice.

"I'm real sorry for all the trouble you've been through because of me. And all the trouble Ted's been through." He shook his head. "You could have been killed."

He looked so unhappy Laura wanted to wrap her arms around him and tell him it was all right. This reaction frightened her almost as much as the fire. She never wanted to feel any tender emotions toward any man other than her brother. Men weren't to be trusted, she reminded herself. "But I wasn't," she replied, adding stiffly, "in fact I owe you my life." The brown of his eyes had softened to a sort of doe color and she was feeling light-headed. Her fear of her own emotions multiplied. "I'm just glad this business is over with," she said with brisk finality. "Now we can all get back to our own lives."

"Yeah," he replied dryly. It was clear from his tone and the sudden coolness that entered his eyes that he took her briskness to mean she wasn't totally ready to forgive him.

Laura started to assure him she held no grudge, but the words died in her throat. It was better this way, she reasoned. She'd made a promise to herself years earlier and her reactions to Frank Davidson were seriously threatening that promise.

"How about the ride?" he asked with terse politeness.

The last thing she wanted was to spend another ten to twelve hours alone with him. "Don't you have to finish the delivery?" she questioned, looking for a polite way to escape his disturbing company. "Surely the police must have found the load you were hauling. Or do they have to hold all that, too?"

He shrugged. "It wasn't a real run, anyway. The crates contained a few concrete blocks to give them weight." Obviously sensing her resistance, he frowned. "Look, I don't blame you if you don't want to spend any more time with me. I just thought sharing a ride would be convenient. But I'll rent you your own car."

As he started to rise, she held up her hand in a halting gesture. She didn't want him to think she was so petty and vindictive that she couldn't even stand his company. But she certainly couldn't confess that the real reason she didn't want to ride with him was because she was experiencing a certain attraction toward him she didn't want to feel. "We can share the ride," she said levelly. "It would be ridiculous for both of us to drive back separately."

The frown on his face softened. "Maybe this will give me a chance to convince you I'm not an ogre."

Watching his departing back, she chewed on the inside of her bottom lip. She'd feel much safer if he was an ogre.

Leaving the table, she found a phone and called Ted to tell him the good news. She felt a prickling on the back of her neck as she hung up and turned to find Frank standing a couple of feet behind her.

"I always seem to catch you on the telephone," he said with a self-conscious grin.

It was a sort of boyish look and it strongly threatened her defenses. "Thought I should call Ted and tell him the good news so he can stop worrying," she said.

The grin disappeared. "Guess he was relieved to learn he'd been cleared."

"Very," she confirmed.

Frank frowned uneasily. "Did he give you any indication about how he was feeling toward me?"

It was easy to see Frank really did care what Ted thought of him. "He wanted me to tell you that he doesn't hold any grudge," she replied. "In fact he wants to know if he can have his old job back when he finishes mending."

Frank smiled with relief. "Sure thing."

A little later, as they left the motel and headed toward Pennsylvania, Frank broke the silence that had again settled between them. "I really am sorry I was so hard on you," he said stiffly. "I know I behaved like a royal pain in the neck."

She glanced toward him. She'd felt a lot safer around him when he was being arrogant, bullheaded, self-righteous and bossy. "You had a lot on your mind," she replied stiffly.

A grimness came over his features. "Yeah, but that doesn't excuse my behavior." His jaw twitched with self-directed anger and he raked his hand through his hair. "Every time I think of how you could have been killed in that fire, I want to kick myself."

There was a protectiveness in his voice that sent a warm current of excitement through her. Fighting it, she said tightly, "I invited myself along."

Reaching over, he combed a wayward strand of her hair away from her face and tucked it behind her ear. "I'm just glad everything worked out okay."

His fingers left a trail of fire across her cheek. "Me, too," she managed to say levelly. Sitting back in her seat, she fought to regain the control she normally had over herself where men were concerned. But it wasn't easy. No other man had ever affected her the way Frank Davidson did. It's just because my nerves have been so much on edge, she assured herself. Once she had time to realize that it was really over and Ted was safe, her equilibrium would return and she'd stop having these acute reactions to the man.

Again a silence descended within the car. But it was not the tense silence that had been between them in the cab of the truck. Instead it was a comfortable silence and that made Laura even more uneasy.

Trying not to think about her companion, she watched the passing scenery. But her will where Frank Davidson was concerned was unusually weak. Covertly she glanced toward him. When he wasn't worried and angry, there was a kindness about his face, and she found herself remembering how protective those brown eyes of his could look. You're only asking for trouble, her little voice warned sternly.

They'd been traveling for nearly an hour when Frank again broke the silence between them. "Now that Ted's been cleared, I suppose you'll be going back to Kansas City," he said in a tone that made it a question.

"Yes. I hate leaving Ted in the hospital, but my boss wasn't real happy about my taking off at a moment's notice. I have to get back as quickly as I can or I might not have a job left." What she didn't add was that she'd feel a lot safer with fifteen hundred miles between her and Frank Davidson.

Frank frowned. "I know Ted will be sorry to see you go."

"It can't be helped," she replied.

"I suppose you have someone special who's impatiently waiting for you to get back, too," he added in a conversational tone.

"No, no one, really," she replied.

Frank glanced toward her and smiled coaxingly. "Then how about letting me take you out to dinner before you leave. I'd like a chance to prove to you that I can be a reasonably nice guy."

Laura's heart skipped a beat. Frank Davidson could charm the fuzz off a peach with that easy drawl and boyish smile. But she was no peach and she didn't want to be charmed. "Thanks, but I really want to spend all my time with my brother until I have to leave."

The smile changed to a frown for a brief moment, then his expression became unreadable. "Guess I can't blame you."

She knew he thought she was really refusing the date because she was still angry with him for having accused Ted in the first place. Again she started to tell him she wasn't, but again the words caught in her throat. It was safer letting him think she was. She called herself a coward as silence fell between them. Better a coward than a fool, she reasoned.

They only stopped for quick meals on the way back. Laura insisted on paying for hers, and their conversation consisted of impersonal comments.

By the time they turned onto the gravel road leading to Frank's place, she knew she'd convinced him she had no interest in spending any time with him. She doubted she'd ever see him again once she picked up Ted's car and left. Which is definitely for the best, she told herself firmly.

Parking in front of the gate, Frank climbed out to unlock it. Night had fallen and he left the headlights of the car on to light his way.

Laura saw him frowning worriedly as he walked back. "What's wrong?" she asked as he slid in behind the wheel.

"Just wondering where Rough and Ready are," he answered, putting the car in gear and driving into the enclosure. A couple of big pole lights illuminated the garage and the path to the house as well as the parking area.

Laura looked around for the dogs, too, as Frank pulled into a spot next to Ted's car. She didn't see them, either. “Maybe they're asleep somewhere,” she suggested as they both climbed out of the rental car.

“They don't usually sleep this time of night,” he replied, moving toward the trunk. Pausing, he again surveyed the enclosure, then whistled for them.

“Those dogs of yours are having a nice little nap,” a man's voice interrupted.

Twisting around, Laura saw a large, brown-haired man coming toward them. In his hand he was carrying a very dangerous-looking automatic pistol. It was pointed at Frank.

“Damn high fence for climbing, too,” the man said grudgingly. “But I didn't want to cut the lock and give you any advance warning of my presence.”

“What are you doing here, Kyle?” Frank demanded.

“You've caused me a lot of trouble, Frank,” Bill Kyle replied. “You,” he said to Laura, “come around here and stand by your boyfriend.”

“Stay where you are, Laura,” Frank ordered.

“I can shoot her now, if you like,” Kyle threatened. “I don't like being disobeyed.”

Laura knew he wasn't making an empty threat. Moving cautiously, she came around the car and took a position next to Frank.

“While I was in prison, all I could think of was how I was going to make you pay,” Kyle said, keeping the gun pointed at Frank. “Now you've made me go and shoot a cop. My life's not worth a red cent. Too bad you saved your lady friend only to bring her back here to face death."

"You've no reason to harm Laura," Frank said gruffly.

Kyle scowled. "You're wrong. I spent two years of my life caged like an animal, kept away from my wife. Before you die, I want you to know what it feels like to worry that you'll never hold your woman again." Kyle laughed. "Only in your case, it'll be the truth."

"Laura's not my girlfriend. She's Ted Martin's sister," Frank pointed out curtly. "The only reason she's here is because she wanted to help her brother. Truth is, she doesn't even like me."

"Nice try," Kyle said with a smile. "But it really doesn't matter. I know you. It wouldn't matter if she hated your guts. You'd feel guilty if she died and I want to see that guilt on your face before I kill you. After what I've lived through because of you, I deserve to see you suffer."

"You brought your misfortune on yourself," Frank growled. Moving suddenly, he stepped in front of Laura.

Kyle grinned maliciously. "That's not going to save her." Addressing Laura, he said, "You'd better step out here, lady, or I'm going to shoot him where he stands."

Laura tried to think past her fear. She could see Frank's muscles tensed for action. What was needed was a diversion. Stepping out from behind Frank, she let out a small yelp and dropped to the ground as if she'd sprained her ankle. For a split second Kyle's full attention went to her. Immediately, Frank sprang at him.

A shot rang out and Laura's breath locked in her lungs. She saw Frank's shoulder jerk, but he managed to grab Kyle before a second shot could be fired.

As the two men struggled, Laura scrambled to her feet. Frank had grabbed the wrist of the hand in which Kyle held the gun.

Both were big men and strong. But there was blood soaking into the arm of Frank's shirt. He'd been shot. That gave Kyle a real advantage. Frantically Laura looked around for a weapon. There was nothing. She poised herself, ready to jump into the fight at the first opportunity. But it wasn't easy to judge. The men were moving and she didn't want to distract Frank and give Kyle even more of an advantage.

Frank hit Kyle's hand against the car. Kyle let out a yell but held on to the weapon. Frank hit the wrist a second time and Kyle dropped the gun.

Without hesitation, Laura weaved around the men and retrieved the revolver. Holding the gun with both hands, the way Ted had taught her, she fired one shot into the air, to get the men's attention, then said, "All right, Mr. Kyle. Just stand where you are and don't make the mistake of thinking I don't know how to use one of these things."

Both men froze momentarily. Then Frank rolled away from Kyle. Moving awkwardly, he rose and went to stand by Laura's side. "I'll watch him. You go call the police,'' he ordered, holding his hand out to take the weapon from her.

As she handed him the gun, Laura's gaze fell on the blood-soaked sleeve of his shirt and she frowned worriedly. ''Will you be all right?''

''It's just a flesh wound,'' he replied. ''Now go.''

She started toward the house, but he called her back. ''The keys are in my pocket,'' he said. ''You'll have to get them out.''

As she reached down into the pocket of his jeans, the hard feel of his muscular thigh beneath her hand sent a rush of excitement radiating up her arm and a warm, hard knot formed in her abdomen. Scowling at herself, she fished out the keys and ran toward the house.

She called for the police and an ambulance, then hurried out to stand by Frank in case he should need her.

The police and ambulance showed up in only minutes.

''You can take a look at my arm in a minute. First, I've got to find my dogs,'' Frank insisted, when the paramedics approached him.

Laura looked again at the blood-soaked sleeve of his shirt and fear for him shook her. ''Let these men do their job,'' she ordered curtly. ''You're not going to be able to help your dogs if you die from loss of blood.''

Frank glanced at his arm. ''I'm not losing that much blood.'' Walking over to his pickup, he took out a large flashlight.

Laura couldn't make herself let him go. Hiding her fear and anxiousness behind a mask of anger, she blocked his path. "You are the most bullheaded man I've ever met. Give me that flashlight. I'll find the dogs while the paramedics look at your arm."

Frank looked hard into her face. "A person could get the idea you don't dislike me as much as you want me to believe," he said gruffly.

Laura's back stiffened. She couldn't let him guess the truth. "You saved my life. I'm not going to repay you by standing by and watching you bleed to death," she replied tersely.

His frown returned. "I'm not going to bleed to death. Now get out of my way so I can find my dogs."

Laura saw a drop of blood drip to the ground and her jaw tensed with determination. "I'm not impressed by your caveman attitude," she snapped. "Now give that flashlight to me and go get your arm bandaged."

"Caveman?" he growled under his breath. For a moment longer Frank hesitated, then grudgingly handed her the light.

Laura couldn't believe she'd talked to him like that. Well, he needed it, she told herself, as she hurried off to find the dogs.

They'd been hidden behind a bush near the edge of the drive. Kneeling beside them, she stroked them lightly and determined that they were still breathing.

"I'll have to get them to the vet," Frank's voice sounded from above her.

"You'll have to sign these papers if you're not going to let us take you to the hospital," a paramedic demanded, coming up behind Frank. He sounded frustrated, and Laura guessed Frank had given the man a difficult time.

"You go to the hospital. I'll take care of the dogs," she ordered.

Frank stood his ground. "I don't need to go to the hospital. It was only a flesh wound and these guys have cleaned it and bandaged it."

"A doctor should examine him and he should probably have some antibiotics just to be safe," the paramedic corrected. "He'll also be wanting some pain medication before morning."

"I'll see a doctor when my dogs have been taken care of," Frank growled. Taking the clipboard from the paramedic, he scrawled his name on the paper.

"Guess I know how you feel," the man admitted, also looking worriedly down at the dogs. "You'll need some help loading them." He waved for one of the policemen and together they lifted the dogs into the back of Frank's pickup while Frank went inside and called the vet to let him know he was on his way.

Laura was kneeling in the bed of the truck, petting the dogs, when Frank returned.

"You better get home and get some rest," he said. "It's been a trying couple of days."

The truth was, she wanted to go home. She wanted to get as far away from Frank as she could. Seeing him hurt was weakening her resolve tremendously. "I should," she said. It was a statement meant more for herself than for him.

Climbing down out of the bed of the truck, she watched Frank cover the dogs with a blanket he'd carried from the house. Then he closed the tailgate. He winced each time he used his injured arm, and she felt a matching sharp pain run through hers.

"I'll drive," she heard herself saying. She couldn't believe she was doing this, but she couldn't just walk away. She held out her hand for the keys.

He tossed her an impatient frown. "There's no need. I can handle this on my own."

"It's a stick shift. You'll need both arms," she pointed out curtly. "And one of them isn't working too good. Now give me those keys."

"I suppose if I don't, you're going to call me bullheaded again and accuse me of having a caveman mentality," he muttered dryly.

"Probably," she conceded.

"You really know how to drive a stick shift?" he asked, continuing to hesitate.

"I'm a little rusty, but I can handle it," she assured him. "Now give me the keys."

Still frowning uncertainly, he handed her the keys.

She was rustier than she thought, Laura discovered. She ground the gears several times before she again got the hang of shifting correctly. Each time, she waited for Frank to make some chauvinistic crack but he didn't.

Dr. Cook was waiting for them when they drove up. Between the three of them, they managed to get the dogs inside. "Now you two go make yourselves comfortable in the waiting room," the vet instructed once the dogs were carefully laid on the examining table. "I'll need to run a few tests."

Wanting distance between herself and Frank, Laura sat in a chair across the room from him. That was as much of a mistake as sitting next to him. From where she was, she could see how tired he looked and read the worry on his face. Unable to stop herself, she rose and crossed to sit beside him. "They're going to be all right," she said comfortingly.

"They were breathing good and strong," he conceded, leaning his head against the wall and closing his eyes.

She could see the pain lines mingling with the worry lines on his face. "You should have gone to the hospital," she scolded tersely.

Keeping his eyes closed, he frowned but said nothing.

It was about half an hour later when the vet came in. "Looks to me like they're going to be just fine," he announced with a yawn. "All they were given was a simple sleeping compound. But I want to keep them here until they wake up so I can make certain there's no side effects."

Frank drew a sigh of relief. "Thanks, doc," he said, levering himself into a standing position.

Again Laura saw him wince and again she felt a jab of pain. Stop it, she ordered herself. But it didn't seem to be anything she had any control over.

She helped the men move the dogs into cages, then adding her thanks to Frank's, she bid the vet goodnight.

Climbing behind the wheel of the pickup, she scowled as she stared out the windshield. As much as she wanted to escape to the solitude of Ted's apartment, she knew she wasn't going to be able to rid herself of Frank's company just yet. "Which way to the hospital?" she asked curtly.

"Just take me home," he replied. "I'll see my doctor tomorrow."

"You'll see a doctor tonight," she snapped. As she turned toward him, her gaze narrowed threateningly. "I'm tired, I'm dirty, and I've had two really bad scares in just over twenty-four hours. I'm in no mood to argue with you. Now how do I get to the hospital from here?"

"I'm not certain which of us is the most bullheaded," he muttered. Still frowning, he sat back in his seat and said, "Turn right."

It was after three in the morning when Laura guided the pickup into its parking space at Frank's place.

"Thanks for all your help," he said groggily.

"You're welcome," she replied. The doctor had given Frank a shot for the pain, and it was obviously making him extremely drowsy. "You better get up to the house and go to bed," she added.

He shook his head. "Need to rechain the fence after you leave." His brow wrinkled deeply as he tried to concentrate. "And I should see you get home safely."

"I can rechain the fence and get myself home just fine," she assured him. "The doctor said you were to go immediately to bed."

Frank rubbed the back of his neck. "I'm going to have to have a talk with him. That shot he gave me was sure strong."

"He wanted you to get some rest," she replied, adding with authority, "now go to bed."

Nodding as if to say he had no will to argue, he started up the path toward the house.

She watched him, and the frown on her face deepened. He was weaving. The doctor had checked to make certain Frank had someone to drive him home before he gave him the pain medication. He'd told Laura it would make Frank a bit drowsy, but clearly Frank was having a much stronger reaction. Catching up with him, she slipped under his arm like a crutch. "Come on, I'll help you get inside."

"I'm sorry for the rough time I gave you," he mumbled gruffly.

"You've already apologized," she replied.

He lowered his head to look at her with drug-fogged eyes. "But you're still angry with me."

Her concern for him was seriously weakening her defenses. "I'm not angry with you," she heard herself admitting. Becoming afraid he was going to fall asleep before she could get him inside, she ordered curtly, "Now be quiet and concentrate on walking."

He squinted in an attempt to focus beyond the fog. "You sound angry and you look angry."

She *was* angry, but not with him. In spite of all her efforts to ignore their close physical contact, her whole body was acutely aware of his. "I'm just tired," she said tersely.

As they entered the house, she brought them to a halt in the entrance hall. For a moment, she considered guiding him into the living room and leaving him on the couch but she knew he needed to be in bed where he would be comfortable. "Which way to the bedroom?" she asked.

"That way." He nodded toward the stairs.

"Great," she muttered, tightening her arm around his waist for an even firmer grip. The imprint of his sturdy musculature burned into her as her leg and hip moved against his. She felt the stirring of desire and fought it.

"I didn't want Ted to be guilty," Frank said as they started up the stairs. "Made me real angry when I found out about the evidence against him. I thought he was my friend."

"He is your friend," Laura assured him.

"Hope so." Frank scowled at himself. "I should've been nicer to you, too. Trouble was, you were so cute. Your eyes get little gold specks in them when you're angry, and you wrinkle your nose just a little." He smiled crookedly at this thought. "I was afraid you might be able to cloud my mind until I couldn't recognize fact from fiction."

"It's all right," she told him, wishing she had a stronger hold on her mind where he was concerned.

Reaching the bedroom, she used the light from the hall to see her way as she helped him into a sitting position on the side of the bed. "I feel real dizzy," he muttered with a frown.

"Just sit there for a minute," she ordered. Quickly she removed his boots. Then she began unbuttoning his shirt. His skin felt incredibly inviting and the desire to run her hands over his shoulders was strong. Hurriedly, she finished removing the garment. Deciding he could sleep with the rest of his clothes on, she said, "Now lie down."

"Yes, ma'am," he replied fuzzily.

Worriedly, Laura glanced at his bandage. There was no fresh blood. Breathing a sigh of relief, she covered him with the bedspread, then escaped into the hall.

Needing a barrier between them, she closed the door of his room, then leaned against the wall and drew a deep breath. His admission that he found her cute played through her mind, and she felt an excited tingle. She trembled as the remembered feel of his body against hers continued to taunt her. Stop it! she ordered herself. She forced herself to remember the way he'd flirted with the waitress at the Twenty-Four Hours Café and a coldness spread over her.

Going to the truck, she found her purse. The two bottles of pills that the doctor had given her were inside it. One contained pain pills to be used as needed. The other held antibiotics, and Frank was to take one of those in three hours.

She frowned at the bottle, then at the house. He'd never wake up on his own to take them, and the doctor had been insistent about his needing them. She knew she had no choice.

Walking down to the gate she pulled it closed and wrapped the chain around the middle poles to hold it closed. But she didn't lock the padlock. She'd need a key to get out if she did that. Besides, the crooks were caught.

Tiredly, she went into the house and up to the bedroom. Other than noting that Frank was sleeping peacefully, she tried to ignore him. There was a radio alarm on the bedside table. Taking it, she went downstairs to the living room and set it up on the coffee table. Then lying down on the couch, she went to sleep.

Chapter Five

When the alarm went off three hours later, Laura forced herself awake.

Going into the kitchen, she found a glass. The doctor had suggested the pills be taken with milk. Hoping Frank had some, she opened the refrigerator. He did. In fact, his refrigerator held a goodly assortment of real food. When she'd opened Ted's refrigerator, all she'd found was some beer, moldy cheese and a jar of peanut butter. She poured the milk, then headed upstairs.

Frank's home was really very nice, she thought as she walked through the living room. It wasn't fancy but the furniture was good quality and obviously bought for comfort. It was very tidy, too. The furniture was even dusted. She wondered if he hired someone to come in and clean or if he had a steady girlfriend who kept his home in such good condition on a voluntary basis. The thought of a girlfriend caused an uneasy pang in the pit of her stomach.

As she tried to ignore the disturbing sensation, her gaze suddenly fell on the fireplace in the living room. It looked exceedingly cozy. To her chagrin, she found herself wondering if Frank did a lot of entertaining of women friends in front of it. In the dead of winter, with snow all around outside, it would certainly be a romantic setting. The pang she'd felt a moment earlier became an uncomfortable twisting in her abdomen. "I do *not* care what he does or who he does it with," she stated aloud as if affirming a vow. Then scowling at herself, she hurried upstairs.

Waking Frank wasn't easy, but finally he opened his eyes.

"Laura?" He frowned at her as if he wasn't quite certain her being there was a dream or reality.

"It's time for your pill," she said sternly.

"Yes, ma'am," he muttered.

Once she was certain he'd swallowed his medicine, she told him to go back to sleep. He nodded as if still in a daze, then turning on his side, he obeyed.

Out in the hall, she raked a hand through her hair. She felt grungy. She needed a shower and a change of clothes. Frowning at the closed bedroom door, she considered going to Ted's place and leaving Frank to fend for himself but she couldn't bring herself to be so callous. He was still really groggy. She'd stick around for six hours, until it was time for his next pill, and then she'd leave.

But she wasn't going to wait for a shower. Going out to the rented car, she retrieved her overnight bag. In addition to the bathroom off the master bedroom, she found a second full bath a little way down the hall between the two guest bedrooms. Leaving her case in one of the adjoining bedrooms, she went in and took a shower. The water felt good but as she washed, she found herself wondering how many other women had used this shower. They probably used the one in the master bedroom, she told herself and again felt the uncomfortable twisting in her stomach. She cursed under her breath. What difference did it make who used what shower in Frank's house? she berated herself. She certainly had no plans to participate in his private life.

Returning to the bedroom, her torso wrapped in one towel and drying her hair with another, she suddenly froze. Frank was standing in the doorway, leaning against the jamb.

"You do look good in a towel," he said, his gaze traveling over her lazily.

Finding her voice, she said stiffly, "You're supposed to be asleep."

"I had this weird dream that a woman with the gentlest, brownest eyes I'd ever seen in my life was forcing medication down my throat. Then I heard water running. My mind's still a little foggy from that shot the doctor gave me, but I thought I should investigate." His gaze rested on her face. "What are you doing here? I had the distinct impression you couldn't wait to get away from me."

She hated the weakness in herself that caused her to feel so shaken by his mere gaze. "I promised the doctor I'd make certain you took your medication," she replied with schooled coldness, making it sound as if her actions had been based solely on a sense of duty. "When we got here, you were really knocked out so I decided I'd better stick around. But now that you're more alert, you can take your medication on your own. So, if you'll just leave and let me get dressed, I'll be on my way."

"Sorry I was so much trouble," he growled sarcastically. Straightening away from the doorjamb, he left, closing the door behind him.

The urge to run after him and tell him he hadn't been any real trouble was strong. But he is trouble, with a capital T, her little voice warned, and she resisted the urge.

Dressing hurriedly, she merely ran a comb through her wet hair. She'd dry it when she got to Ted's place. Right now, she just needed to get out of Frank's house. But as she left the room and started down the hall, she heard water running in the bathroom in the master bedroom. It sounded as if Frank was taking a shower.

She shrugged and told herself not to pay any attention. But at the foot of the stairs, she came to an abrupt halt. He was still groggy. He might fall. Then there was his wound. If he got the bandage wet, it would have to be changed.

She wished she was more callous but she wasn't. "He did save my life," she reminded herself.

Leaving her suitcase by the door, she went upstairs. Standing in the hall outside his bedroom door, she waited until she heard the water stop and heard him moving around in the bedroom. Then she knocked on the door.

He was clothed only in a towel wrapped around his lower torso when he opened the door.

"We've really got to stop meeting like this," she muttered, the sight of his broad, dark-haired chest causing her blood to race.

He greeted her presence with an impatient scowl. "I thought you left."

"I was worried you might get your bandage wet," she replied stiffly. "And I figured that if you did, you wouldn't be able to change it on your own."

The frown on his face deepened. "Look, I'm not interested in this Florence Nightingale routine. It's clear you want to get out of here. So just go. I can take care of myself."

"I do want to get out of here," she admitted honestly. "But I promised the doctor I'd look after you and I keep my promises. So why don't you just let me change your bandage, then I can leave."

For a moment he looked as if he was going to throw her out if she didn't leave on her own, then his expression became shuttered and he gave an indifferent shrug with his good shoulder. "Suit yourself. There's bandages in the bathroom cabinet."

He was sitting in a chair by the window holding a pair of scissors when she returned to the bedroom.

As she started to unwrap the arm, he winced. "I think I should get you a pain pill," she said.

He caught her wrist as she started toward the nightstand beside the bed. "No, thanks. I don't like being lost in a fog."

Even with the anger between them, his touch had a disconcerting effect. "Fine," she said, jerking free. His scowl darkened and she wished she'd been less dramatic about freeing herself.

"You lie well," he said, his jaw tight with pain as she carefully unwrapped the wound.

"What?" she demanded curtly.

"I have this vague recollection of you telling me you weren't angry with me," he elaborated through clenched teeth. "That you didn't blame me for suspecting your brother."

"I don't."

His jaw tightened even more. "Then it's just me in general you don't like."

"I don't have any feelings about you one way or another," she informed him, wishing this were true and again assuring herself it would be as soon as she had time to regain her equilibrium. "However, you did save my life and I made a promise to the doctor. So I feel an obligation toward your health."

He fell silent until she finished rebandaging his wound. But the moment she was done, he said with dismissal, "Now you can consider your debt fully paid."

"I want to," she replied. "But first I need your word that you'll take your pills. The times are on the bottle."

"I'll take my pills," he assured her coolly.

"I moved your alarm downstairs. I'll get it." She left the room and raced downstairs. She just wanted to be away from this man as quickly as possible.

"You can show yourself out," he said when she returned a couple of minutes later. He was ordering her out of his house, and she told herself she was glad to be going.

"It's been a real adventure knowing you, Mr. Davidson," she replied briskly and left.

Outside, she drew a deep breath. It was over. Ted was safe and she didn't have to have anything more to do with Frank Davidson.

Going to Ted's apartment, she crawled into bed and slept.

It was midafternoon when she woke. After pouring herself some orange juice, she dialed Harriet Ownen's number. She didn't really want to talk to her. Harriet was her supervisor at work, and none of the employees liked her. Harriet had come up through the ranks and enjoyed her sense of power now that she had reached a position where she could tell the others what to do.

"You know you left at a very inconvenient time," Harriet said in her strongest reprimanding tone when she discovered it was Laura on the other end of the line.

"It was an emergency," Laura replied in her defense.

"Well, we're having an emergency here," Harriet stated, her tone implying that Laura's emergency was of no real importance. "We're having another cutback and I'm afraid that if you're not at your desk by nine sharp tomorrow morning, you'll be getting a pink slip."

Laura considered arguing that she had seniority but she knew that wouldn't do any good. Harriet wanted her to beg. Well, she wasn't going to. "Then I guess you'll just have to give me a pink slip," she heard herself saying and slammed down the phone. In the next instant, a wave of insecurity shook her and she grabbed the receiver, intending to call Harriet back and apologize. Then more slowly, she replaced it. Life at work had been miserable since Harriet had become her supervisor. She'd been thinking about quitting for months and finding a new job. "And this is as good a time as any," she announced to the empty apartment.

Feeling relieved that she would never have to face Harriet's disapproving looks again, she dressed in slacks and a sweater and went to the hospital to visit with Ted.

"Maybe you could get a job here and live with me," he suggested when she told him about quitting.

"I've got the farm," she said, remembering the day her mother had insisted on putting the family home in Laura's name. *A woman needs a roof over her head,* Evelyn Martin had said. *You have to have something to count on in this life. You sure can't count on a man.* Laura had been worried about how Ted would react, but he hadn't minded. *You helped Mom pay the bills while I was still in school and you've taken care of her. You deserve to have it,* he'd said. *Besides, this way, I know I'll always have a place to come back to.*

Laura frowned. *A place to come back to.* Sometimes the farm felt like an albatross around her neck when all the bad memories returned to haunt her.

"Then how about finding a temporary job here and sticking around until I'm back on my feet?" he coaxed. "I really like having you around. It'll keep me from going crazy in this bed."

"I thought that cute blond nurse was doing that," she said with a smile, remembering the bantering she'd heard between her brother and the woman when she'd entered.

"Carol is a distraction," he admitted. "But I really like having my sister here."

"Well, maybe I could apply at one of those temporary agencies," she agreed. "If I go back to K.C., I'll just worry about you."

Ted beamed. "Great!"

"Good to hear you sounding so well," Frank said from the doorway. Then seeing Laura, he came to an abrupt halt. "I'll come back later."

"No, wait," Ted called out, stopping Frank before he could make his exit complete. As Frank stood stiffly by the door, Ted's gaze traveled from Frank to Laura, then back to Frank. "What's the hurry?"

"No hurry. Just didn't want to interrupt your visit with your sister," Frank replied in an easy drawl. But although he tried to sound casually friendly, there was an edge of coldness in his voice.

Ted glanced toward Laura, then turned to Frank. "Look, Frank, if Laura's been a bit testy with you, just ignore it. She doesn't really mean it. Where men are concerned, she's—"

"Ted," Laura said warningly through clenched teeth.

"She just has a hard time getting used to new people," he finished, tossing her an impatient glance. "I was hoping the two of you might be friends."

Laura shifted uneasily as Frank studied her narrowly.

"In fact, I was hoping you might help her find a temporary job," Ted continued coaxingly. "She's agreed to stay until I'm back on my feet."

Frank frowned indecisively as his gaze shifted from Laura to Ted and back to Laura. Then his jaw tensed with decision. "As a matter of fact, I can help. I could use a full-time secretary. Sally's all settled in her new job, and Maryann doesn't want to work full-time. I'm going to have to start driving again until I can build my business up to where I can hire drivers for all the hauls.

In the meantime, I'll need someone to take over the office and keep things running smoothly. 'Course, there'll be a bit of bookkeeping, too, but it's relatively simple."

Laura's whole body tensed. She couldn't work for Frank Davidson! "I really don't know anything about the trucking business."

Frank studied her coolly. "All you'll have to do is keep an accurate schedule, do a little typing and filing and, if you're as sharp as Ted is always telling me you are, I can teach you the bookkeeping in a few hours."

"Ted brags a lot," she muttered.

"You can do it," Ted encouraged.

"It'll give me a chance to make up for not having more faith in Ted," Frank added tersely. "And if you're hesitating because of my presence, you don't have to worry. I won't be around much at all."

Laura felt trapped. Frank had made it perfectly clear he was offering her this job as an apology to Ted. He was even assuring her he had no personal interest where she was concerned. There was no polite way out of this.

"Of course, she'll take the job," Ted said, tossing her a reproving glance when she remained silent.

"Sure, why not," she agreed with schooled nonchalance. This could even turn out to be a good thing, she reasoned, trying to look on the bright side. Working for Frank, she was certain to be exposed to his faults so often that the attraction she felt for him would die a swift death.

* * *

But a couple of hours later she was questioning her judgment. When visiting hours were over, Frank had said his arm was bothering him and asked her if she'd mind starting to work for him immediately. "I could use some help picking up the dogs," he explained.

"Sure," she'd agreed, suddenly frightened by how much she honestly wanted to help him.

She'd followed him to his place. As they drove up, a woman who looked to be in her mid-fifties came out of the office. She had a baby in one arm and was holding on to a toddler with her free hand.

"Maryann, this is Laura Martin." Frank made quick introductions as he and Laura met the woman halfway across the parking area. "She's going to be taking over Sally's job."

"Martin?" Maryann eyed Laura with interest. "Ted's sister?"

"That right," Laura confirmed, wishing she didn't feel so relieved to learn Maryann was not a tall, slinky blonde.

Maryann gave her a friendly smile. "Nice to meet you." Then as the toddler pulled on her arm, her expression became anxious and she turned her attention to Frank. "My daughter had an emergency," she explained. "Her six-year-old fell and cut himself pretty deep. She thinks he might have a broken wrist, too. She dropped these two off here on her way to the hospital. Her husband's out of town and my Sam took your short run to Gettysburg." She looked up at Frank beseechingly. "I should really be at the hospital with her."

"Go," he said, taking the baby in his good arm.

"You'll find everything you need in the satchel in the office, and there's a couple of calls you should return," Maryann said, placing the toddler's hand in Frank's.

Immediately the little girl sat down on the gravel drive and began to cry.

Laura saw Frank wince. It was his injured arm that was being pulled. She winced with him. Moving quickly, she picked the child up, freeing Frank. For a moment the little girl was startled into silence, then with a wail resumed her crying.

"I'm afraid Cathy is a little cranky," Maryann apologized over her shoulder as she headed for her car. "She didn't get her nap today." Climbing into the car, she yelled, "Be back as quickly as I can."

Laura turned to Frank as the car disappeared down the drive. The baby's face was screwing up in preparation for a crying fit. "Joey, we men have to stick together," Frank addressed him sternly. "Now be quiet and let me make my calls." He started bouncing the baby lightly in his arm while he talked to him, and Joey's face relaxed into a grin. "Good boy," Frank said with a relieved smile and started toward the office.

Watching him, Laura couldn't believe his knack or his confidence in handling the baby. She also couldn't believe he'd volunteered to take care of two children without blinking an eye. The only other man she'd even known who would've done such a thing was Neil Howard, who owned the place next to hers. But he and his wife had eight kids of their own.

Her musings, however, were cut short by Cathy's continued wailing. "Okay, what do you like to do for entertainment?" she asked. She didn't really expect an answer. It was a rhetorical question, meant more for herself than the child.

"Frank," the little girl said through her sobs, extending her arms toward the office.

"He seems to be able to charm them at all ages," Laura muttered, shifting Cathy into a more comfortable position in her arms and walking toward the office.

Entering, she found Frank on the phone. Joey had fallen half asleep but Cathy's crying caused his eyes to pop open.

"Hold on a minute," Frank said to the person at the other end of the line. Turning to Laura, he tossed her his keys. "Take her up to the house and feed her or something." It was a definite "get out of here with that crying child" order.

For a moment Laura's back stiffened. This hadn't been her doing. Then she saw him glance toward the phone worriedly. He had a business to rebuild. Quickly she turned and left. Immediately, Cathy began to sob more violently.

Entering the house, Laura headed for the kitchen. She'd baby-sat for the Howards' children many times, and food always seemed to help with a crying child. "How about something to eat?" she suggested encouragingly.

Cathy stopped crying and looked around. "Apple," she said, pointing toward the counter.

Laura saw some apples in a bowl and breathed a sigh of relief. Setting the child on the floor, she began to peel and slice the fruit. To her relief Cathy remained standing beside her, watching silently.

Then, carrying the child and the cut-up apple into the den, she switched on the television and found some cartoons to entertain the little girl while she ate.

Frank came in about half an hour later. "Sorry I barked at you," he apologized with gruff self-consciousness. "I'm a little short on patience these days."

"It's all right," she replied, wishing he hadn't apologized. She had taken this job to find his faults. Then she frowned. He'd carried the baby's satchel, stuffed full of baby paraphernalia, from his office with his wounded arm and the pain lines were etched deeply into his face. "I would have gone down and gotten the satchel," she scolded curtly. "You've got to be more careful with that arm. You're going to open the wound again."

He glanced toward her. "I appreciate your concern," he said in a voice that suggested he didn't think it was totally honest.

Her jaw tightened defensively. She knew he had a rather low opinion of her. It was safer that way. But she didn't like him thinking she was totally cold-blooded. "I don't like to see anyone in pain," she said stiffly.

"Then maybe you'll take Joey," he suggested in a tone that was more of an order than a request. "Even as light as he is, my arm is beginning to feel as if it might become permanently bent in this position if I don't stretch it soon."

Rising quickly, Laura took the baby. He made a few cooing sounds, but didn't wake up as she settled into the rocking chair with him cradled in her arms.

Frank stretched his arm several times, then settled into one of the large, overstuffed chairs. Immediately, Cathy crawled into his lap.

He looks really comfortable in this setting, Laura thought grudgingly. This wasn't the picture she wanted to paint of Frank Davidson in her mind. It was much too dangerous, considering the attraction she was already fighting.

She dropped her eyes to the baby in her lap. He looked so peaceful and so cuddly. Deep within her, the desire to have a family threatened to emerge from where she'd buried it. Very gently she stroked the baby's cheek. But to have a family meant letting herself fall in love, and she never intended to allow herself to do that. She'd seen the kind of pain and humiliation a man could cause a woman. Feeling an uncomfortable prickling, she looked up to discover Frank studying her.

"You were looking wistful," he said.

"I was just thinking how innocently children view the world and how harsh the reality is when it hits." Shocked that she had been so open about her real thoughts, she dropped her gaze to the baby.

Frank's gaze narrowed as he studied her more closely. "That's a very cynical outlook on life."

"I prefer to think of it as realistic," she replied stiffly. Determined to change the subject, she let her gaze shift to Cathy who had fallen asleep cradled against Frank's arm. "These children seem to feel very comfortable around you."

"Maryann has brought them in several times when I needed her to work and she'd already agreed to baby-sit for her daughter. They're used to me," he said absently. Continuing to study her with an unnerving intensity, he asked gently, "Was reality really that harsh, Laura?"

"Yes," she admitted. She was shocked by her openness. Her mouth formed a hard, warning line as if to say back off, you're getting too close as she turned her gaze away from him abruptly.

For the next hour, only the sound of the nightly news filled the room. Finally a knock on the door interrupted the tense silence that had settled between them. It was Maryann coming for the children.

"Davy only needed stitches," she said in answer to Frank's inquiry about the injured child. "His wrist was only sprained."

A few minutes later, Laura was standing in the wide parking area watching the woman drive off. All she wanted to do was to help Frank get his dogs and then go home. This wasn't working out at all as she'd planned. So far all she'd seen were Frank's good qualities, and her nerves were on a brittle edge.

"Now that you've gotten the gears ground down to the way you like them, you drive," Frank said, tossing her the keys to his pickup.

It had taken twenty-four hours, she thought acidly, but he'd finally made a crack about her driving. It was a relief. She'd been looking for faults. But as she glanced up to glare at him, she saw a mischievous gleam in his eyes. He was joking with her. The temptation to smile back was too strong to resist.

"You should smile more often," he said softly, reaching up and tracing the line of her jaw with the tip of his fingers.

Laura's breath locked in her lungs as she found herself feeling suddenly lost in the soft brown depths of his eyes. Nervously, her teeth closed over her bottom lip. He was dangerously charming. Frightened, her smile changed to a frown as she pulled away from his touch. "We'd better get going," she said coolly, opening the door of the cab and climbing inside.

Seating himself in the passenger's seat, he regarded her musingly. "You're a very uptight lady. You should learn to relax, maybe even laugh. Laughter is supposed to be very good for your health."

Considering her reactions to him, relaxing around him could be very *bad* for her health, she countered mentally. Aloud she said nothing. Chewing on her bottom lip, she concentrated on her driving.

The dogs seemed as happy to see her as they were to see Frank. "They probably remember your voice from when you talked to them last night," he said in an easy, friendly drawl as he opened the tailgate and the dogs jumped up into the back of the truck. "When we get home, you can feed them. After that they'll be your friends for life."

Glancing toward Frank, Laura found herself wondering if he could be as faithful as his pets. Down deep inside, she knew all men were not untrustworthy. The problem was knowing which ones were and which ones weren't. The safe thing to do is to assume they are all untrustworthy, she told herself curtly and turned her attention to the dogs. Giving each animal a gentle scratch behind the ear, she shook her head. "I like them. But they're not very good watchdogs."

"They scared you the first time you saw them," he reminded her with a grin, adding seriously, "I wouldn't want dogs around that might actually harm someone."

Laura drew a tired breath. Frank Davidson really was a very good-hearted man. But being concerned about the safety of others didn't mean he would be faithful to a woman, she warned herself. Determined to keep her thoughts in the proper perspective, she again forced herself to recall his flirtatious exchange with the waitress at the Twenty-Four Hours Café. She glanced toward him. He would certainly have no trouble finding plenty of women who would be attracted to him. A cold chill shook her and she climbed into the cab and concentrated on her driving.

When they arrived at the garage, she fed the dogs while Frank called a couple of his regular drivers and set up runs.

In spite of the fact that he was in business again, as she entered his office to make arrangements for the following day, she saw the worry lines on his face. "What time do you want me here tomorrow?" she asked after he'd hung up the second call.

"I'm an early riser," he replied. "How about eight? And you can consider yourself finished by two so you can go visit your brother."

"I'll see you then," she said. Anxious to be away from his unnerving company, she headed swiftly toward the door. But as she reached for the handle, she came to a stop. "Would you like me to drive you someplace for dinner?" she heard herself asking.

He looked surprised.

He's no more surprised than I am, she thought, wondering what insanity had prompted this offer. She wanted desperately to get away from him and here she was offering to take him to dinner.

"I'll buy," he said, levering himself into a standing position.

He looked even more exhausted than he had a moment earlier, and she frowned worriedly. "You look as if you'd fall asleep trying to read the menu." Then before she even realized the thought had formed in her mind, she heard herself saying, "I noticed you have a fairly well-stocked refrigerator. Why don't I cook up something here?" Again she saw the surprise on his face and again she wondered what insanity had taken hold of her senses. Feeling a need to justify this suggestion, she added, "I did promise the doctor I'd keep an eye on you."

"Wouldn't want the doctor accusing you of not keeping your promise," he said, studying her with interest as he accepted her offer.

All the way up to his house she scolded herself. You're playing with fire, she warned as she fried bacon and scrambled eggs while he set the table and made toast. She'd intended to keep a very safe distance between herself and Frank Davidson, and yet here she was in his kitchen cooking him a meal.

"Ted thinks a lot of you," Frank said, breaking the uneasy silence between them.

"I think a lot of him," she replied. Then determined that the conversation would not revolve around her and Ted, she said, "I understand you have several brothers and sisters."

"One brother and two sisters," he corrected. Setting glasses of orange juice on the table, he studied her levelly. "I know Ted worries about you living alone."

"He doesn't need to worry," she assured him. "I am perfectly capable of taking care of myself." Pausing as she started to set the plates of food on the table, she glanced toward him, her manner businesslike. "Why don't you tell me what my job will entail." Both her expression and her tone made it clear she didn't want the conversation remaining on a personal level.

Sitting down, he studied her for a long moment as if weighing the consequences of ignoring the warning. Then giving in to her wishes, he began to explain the trucking business to her.

When the meal was over, he insisted on drying the dishes while she washed. "I have to exercise my arm to get the stiffness out," he said. "I'll be needing full use of it for driving in a couple of days."

The thought of him with his injured arm behind the wheel of a semi caused a wave of anxiety to wash over her. She glanced toward him. Tiredness had worn down her defenses and the anxiousness she was feeling was obvious in her expression. "Maybe you should give your arm a little more time to heal."

"My arm will be all right," he assured her. His eyes softened. "But it's nice to know you really care."

Furious with herself for letting her guard down so fully, she turned her gaze away from him. "I'm just being practical," she said stiffly. "If you have an accident, the business will collapse and both Ted and I will be out of work."

"Yeah," he muttered. There was impatience in his voice that indicated he wasn't enjoying the way she blew hot then cold. Laying the towel aside, he said tersely, "I'm really tired. Just leave the rest. My cleaning lady comes in the morning and she'll finish."

Laura knew she was being thrown out again but she didn't mind. She'd already made several slips. She didn't want to stick around and make another. "Fine," she replied, wringing out the dishrag, drying her hands and then leaving.

She was halfway to her car when he caught up with her. "I forgot to thank you for the meal," he said stiffly. "You're as good a cook as Ted says you are."

She saw the apology in his eyes and knew he was trying to make amends for ordering her out of his house. Her defenses wavered once again. Frightened by her weakness toward this man, she wanted the anger to remain between them. She needed the barrier. "You're welcome," she replied crisply, then again started toward her car, but he laid a hand on her arm.

"I want you to call me when you get home." It was an order. "With Ted in the hospital, I feel I'm responsible for you."

Her back stiffened. The last thing she wanted was for Frank to take on the role of a big brother. "You're not responsible for me."

His hold on her arm tightened. "Okay, I'm not responsible for you," he conceded gruffly. "Just humor me. Call me when you get home so I won't have to drive over to Ted's place to make certain you're safe."

His touch was having a strongly disconcerting effect on her. "You're being ridiculous," she muttered.

His jaw hardened with resolve. "Either you agree to call me or I'm following you home."

He looked so tired, and she knew he wasn't making an idle threat. "All right. I'll call," she agreed.

Driving home, she felt frustrated. She'd worked very hard to keep a barrier around herself where men were concerned. But Frank Davidson seemed to be able to penetrate it without any effort. While she hated admitting it, she'd felt pleased to discover he had a housekeeper and it wasn't a girlfriend who kept his home in order.

"Men are not to be trusted," she informed the interior of the car. "Especially smooth-talking ones with an easy drawl and a boyish smile." I'm just letting Frank get to me because I've been so off balance these past few days, she reasoned frantically. Having someone try to kill you twice in a little over twenty-four hours would cause anyone to be a bit rattled.

Her chin tightened. But now that things were back to normal, she'd get her emotions in order. She wouldn't play the fool for any man. She liked her life just fine as it was and no man, not even Frank Davidson, was going to find his way into her heart.

Still, to her chagrin, her hand felt a little unsteady as she dialed Frank's number a few minutes later. "I'm here," she said in businesslike tones when he answered. "Be sure you take your pill, and I'll see you in the morning." Without waiting for him to respond, she hung up.

But later as she lay in bed, the memory of him carrying her out of the burning room and the safety she'd felt in his arms taunted her. "There is no safety in a man's arms," she told herself curtly. Drawing a terse breath, she assured herself she would be much more in control after a good night's sleep.

Chapter Six

But a good night's sleep didn't prepare her for the next morning. Frank was waiting for her when she arrived. Going into his office, he had her sit at the desk and, after pulling out various record-keeping books, he went over the ledgers with her. His manner was polite and businesslike. The problem was he stood beside the chair, leaning a little over her shoulder, and his breath was warmly tantalizing as it teased her neck and face. But even worse was the heat of his body as his shoulder and arm brushed against her.

You're behaving like a schoolgirl with her first crush, she chided her body. But that didn't stop its acute awareness of the man.

By noon, her nerves were on a brittle edge.

"I'd say you know as much about my record keeping as I do," Frank said finally, straightening and stretching.

Thank goodness that's over, she sighed mentally. Aloud, she said, "I just hope I can remember it all."

"How about some lunch?" he suggested. "I've got sandwich fixings up at the house and something cold to drink."

"I brought my own," she replied, nodding toward the brown paper bag near her purse.

"Suit yourself," he said with an indifferent shrug and left.

Well, you don't have to worry about him making any passes, she told herself. It's clear he's given up on you. The thought should have brought a sense of relief, but it didn't.

Drawing a shaky breath, she ate her lunch while she went over the record books another time to make certain she understood them. But like a thorn in a rose bush, Frank Davidson remained always in the back of her mind. Like a person waiting for a second shoe to drop, she waited for him to return. But he didn't.

She organized the desk to suit her, went through the mail and arranged it in order of importance, then began filing the mounds of material that had gathered around the office.

"And this place needs a good dusting, too," she muttered, as she stooped to return a folder to a bottom drawer.

"I've been trying to get down here for ages," a female voice said from behind her. "But Frank's always telling me I shouldn't touch anything here unless he's around. He's afraid I might lose something in this mess. And he's been so busy trying to catch those crooks, he ain't been around much."

Rising and turning, Laura found herself face to face with a slightly plumpish woman in her late forties. The woman's dark hair was heavily streaked with gray, but her blue eyes gave no indication of tiredness or age. They were bright as a child's and filled with curiosity.

"I'm Reva McLoyd." The woman wiped her hand on her slacks before extending it toward Laura. "I come by and clean for Frank once a week."

"I'm Laura Martin," Laura introduced herself as she brushed the dust off her hands and accepted the woman's handshake.

"Ted's sister." The woman nodded, smiling broadly. "I can see the family resemblance. I'm real glad your brother's been proved innocent. Just couldn't believe a boy with such laughing brown eyes could be a thief. Though he did look right guilty when he ran." This last thought brought a frown to Reva's face and she shook her head.

"I'm just glad it's over," Laura replied.

Reva bobbed her head in a confirming nod. "Now maybe life can get back to normal around here." Her gaze traveled around the office. "If you're going to be around for a while, I'll give this place a good once over."

Laura glanced at her watch. It was already two. Then she looked at the stack of filing on her desk. "Sure," she said. Calling Ted, she told him she'd be in to see him during the evening visiting hours.

"To tell you the truth, I was right worried about Frank," Reva said as she began to dust. "I used to fuss at him all the time about working too hard and then he almost lost everything. 'Course, he's a strong man. He'd have come back. He doesn't let much get him down for long."

Laura remembered the determination she'd seen in Frank's eyes. "He doesn't strike me as a man who'd give up easily," she said.

"No, ma'am." Reva shook her head sharply. Pausing as she started to attach the wand to the vacuum cleaner, she turned to face Laura. "But this robbery business was hard on him. And then it looked like your brother was guilty. I don't think I've ever seen Frank so upset. I'll tell you what I think. I think he needs a wife, someone who'll treat him special. We all need a soft touch when times are rough."

"I suppose," Laura admitted. She recalled how comforting Frank's arms had been when she'd woken in terror during the night. Then without warning she found herself wishing she could have been here to comfort him when he needed comforting. Don't even think about that, she ordered herself.

"Right," Reva was saying firmly. "What he needs is a wife."

"I keep telling you that I'm waiting until you're free," Frank said, coming in at that moment.

Reva scowled at him. "This is no joking matter. Just look at you. Who's going to rebandage that arm tonight and cook you a decent meal?"

Laura had to bite her tongue to keep from volunteering.

"If I need some help, I can find someone to help me," Frank replied.

Reva's eyes sparkled. "Guess you could," she said knowingly. "I know several eligible females who'd gladly come over here at a moment's notice. Wouldn't be surprised if a couple show up without an invite."

Laura's whole body suddenly felt cold as she pictured Frank with a bevy of women seeing to his every need. The barriers he'd so easily broken were now again firmly in place and reinforced with a heavy layer of ice. I was right, she congratulated herself. It had taken less than a day for her to put Frank Davidson in the proper perspective.

"Thought you'd be gone by now," he said, turning his attention to her.

Laura met his gaze with a cool, businesslike manner. "Mrs. McLoyd—"

"Reva," Mrs. McLoyd corrected with a friendly smile.

"Reva," Laura began again, "wanted to clean and there was a lot of filing to do so I called Ted and told him I'd see him this evening."

"Whatever schedule suits you best," he replied with a nonchalant shrug, and as Reva turned on the vacuum cleaner, he left.

Later as Laura drove to the hospital to visit Ted, the confident expression had returned to her face. She was in control of her world once again.

"How did the new job go today?" Ted asked after a welcoming hug.

"It went very well," she informed him.

His eyes danced with mischief. "And how are you and Frank getting along?"

She knew that look. He was matchmaking. "We get along just fine for a boss and his employee."

Ted frowned. "Frank's really a great guy. If you'd give him half a chance, you'd learn that."

Frank's admission that he could find a woman whenever he needed one played through Laura's mind. "I know all I want to know about Mr. Frank Davidson."

Ted drew a terse breath. "I worry about you, Laura. You keep too much bottled up inside. You have to let go of the past."

"And set myself up to be hurt the way our mother was hurt?" she demanded curtly. "No, thanks."

"Laura, our mother was a very naive woman," Ted pointed out in reasoning tones.

"And how do I know I won't be just as naive?" she demanded.

"Has it ever occurred to you that maybe our mother really didn't want to know the truth?" Ted questioned.

Laura had considered many possibilities but that didn't make her any more confident about her own ability to choose a man who could be trusted. "I really don't want to talk about this," she said tightly.

"Someday you're going to have to talk about it before it eats you away inside and leaves you all hollow," he warned.

"I'd rather be hollow than a fool," she replied. "Now unless you can change the subject, I'm leaving."

Bowing to her demand, Ted suggested a game of gin rummy.

It was late when Laura left the hospital. Because Ted didn't have a roommate at the moment and since he'd been so restless over the past few days, the nurses allowed her to stay and play cards with him until well past the regular visiting hours.

As she drove away, Ted's warning came back to haunt her. "It's better to be safe than sorry," she told herself curtly. Pulling into a market that was open all night, she went inside and bought a chocolate bar. But after one bite, she put it aside. Even chocolate couldn't help this uneasy mood she was in.

In spite of her newly acquired coldness toward Frank Davidson, she found herself glancing toward his place as she drove by. The gate was open, and she guessed he'd called one of his women friends over to see to his needs. The glacier around her emotions thickened even more.

Then she noticed that one of the trucks was parked under a pole light. The hood was up and someone was working on it. Even without a clear view, she knew it was Frank.

Go home, she ordered herself, but instead she turned the car around and went back.

The dogs rushed up to greet her as she parked and climbed out of the car. She glanced around. There were no strange cars on the lot.

"Forget something?" Frank asked irritably, looking down at her from his position above the engine.

Yes, to stay home, she answered mentally, his attitude making her feel like a nuisance. This was a real mistake. Every instinct told her that. Leave! she ordered herself. Instead she heard herself saying, "I thought you were going to consult your little black book and have a friend over to cook your dinner and rebandage your arm." His gaze became shuttered as he studied her narrowly. Why hadn't she just lied, pretended to have left something in the office, gone in there for a minute, come out and left? she berated herself.

"Had to get this truck in shape for a run tomorrow," he replied. He glanced at his watch. "You're out pretty late."

"They let me stay past visiting hours to keep Ted entertained," she explained. Get out of here, her little voice ordered. Obeying, she headed for her car. "I'll be seeing you in the morning. Just wanted to make certain nothing was wrong."

"Yeah," he muttered, following her movements with a speculative frown.

She was climbing into her car when he suddenly climbed down from the short ladder he had been using to see into the engine and came toward her. "As long as you're here," he said, catching the door before she could pull it closed. "I'm having some difficulty replacing the fan belt. My arm's giving me some trouble." He nodded toward the left arm, where the bullet had passed through. "And it seems that I need two good arms for the job. I was wondering if you'd mind giving me a little help."

What she wanted to do was to get away as quickly as possible. But that would make her look as if she were running scared. Which would be the truth, her little voice pointed out. As sturdy as she thought her barrier against him was, the exhaustion etched on his face was threatening it. "Sure," she said with schooled nonchalance. Climbing out of the car, she walked over to the ladder.

"You'll have to climb up." Dragging a crate over to the truck, Frank stepped onto it so he could stand beside her.

"Be careful and don't hurt yourself," he warned as she followed his instructions. The protectiveness in his voice threatened to penetrate the wall of ice she had so carefully constructed. Then there was her traitorous body. At one point his shoulder brushed against hers and in spite of the barrier she had so firmly in place, tiny sparks of heat shot down her arm. Determinedly, she concentrated on getting the job done.

"That should do it," he announced at last and Laura drew a relieved breath.

Climbing down from the crate, he watched her as she came down the ladder, then handed her a rag to wipe her hands off on. "I appreciate the help."

Say thank you and leave, her little voice ordered. But the weariness in his eyes and the drawn look of his face pulled at her. The urge to take him inside, feed him and tuck him into bed was incredibly strong. Cursing the weakness he caused in her, she reminded herself of the conversation between him and Reva. "Next time you should call one of your lady friends. You could've had a hot dinner and someone to help you," she said.

"I don't believe in imposing on others," he replied.

"I'm sure they wouldn't have considered it an imposition," she heard herself saying, then wished she hadn't spoken as his gaze searched her features with an intensity that made her afraid he might see her weakness for him.

"I don't believe in leading on a woman, either," he said evenly. "You ask a woman over to cook dinner for you and nurse you back to health and she might get the impression you're considering a more permanent commitment."

They were standing close and in spite of her best efforts not to react to him, Laura was acutely aware of his masculinity. Even worse, she found herself wanting to move closer. Fighting this destructive urge, she grabbed onto his last words. "And you're a man who doesn't believe in permanent commitments," she elaborated coolly, causing the barrier that was threatening to crumble to again become solid.

"I didn't say that," he corrected, his gaze locking on hers. "What I said was I wasn't interested in any permanent commitment with any of the women I knew I could call."

Suddenly afraid of losing herself in the dark inviting depths of his eyes, she jerked her gaze away. He seemed to have a knack for destroying her guard. "I really have to be going," she said, backing away from him.

But as she reached out to hand him the rag she was still holding, he caught her hand. Taking a step toward her, he placed his free hand under her chin and forced her to look him in the face. "You confuse me, Laura," he said, studying her tiredly. "You're constantly telling me you don't want to be around me any more than you have to and yet you're always here when I need help."

"Just coincidence," she assured him. His touch heated her skin. But it was his gaze that was having the most destructive effect on her. She fought against it, but like a swimmer caught in a whirlpool too strong to resist, she found herself drawn into the dark depths of his eyes.

"Then I'm grateful for coincidences," he replied softly.

His mouth was moving toward hers. She ordered herself to turn away, but her body refused to obey.

The kiss began very gently as if he wanted to savor the soft feel of her lips. Again she ordered herself to jerk free but the feel of his lips on hers was too tantalizing to resist. The blood raced hot through her veins, and her legs felt weak. When she didn't resist, he drew her into his arms, and the kiss became more possessive. For the first time, desire awakened within her. It began as a low, smoldering ember taunting her with its heat, then suddenly it burst into a raging fire threatening to consume her. Shocked by the intensity of her response to this man, fear filled her. Abruptly, she began to fight for her freedom.

Releasing her, Frank frowned down at her in confusion. Reading the fear on her face, his expression softened. "You don't need to be afraid of me, Laura," he said.

Pride demanded that she tell him she wasn't, but the lie refused to be said. Instead, she took a step back, then meeting his gaze, she said shakily, "Please, don't ever do that again."

He studied her with concern. Reaching toward her, he caught her chin in his hand. "I promise you, I will never do anything to harm you."

With every fiber of her being she wanted to believe him but her fear was too great. "Just stay away from me, please." She meant this to come out as an order but instead it sounded more like a plea. Pulling away from him, she walked quickly toward Ted's car. To her relief he didn't follow or try to stop her. As she drove away, she glanced in her rearview mirror. He was standing watching her drive away, a frown of confusion on his face.

"I made a real fool out of myself tonight," she mused unhappily as she entered Ted's apartment. She promised herself it would never happen again.

But later as she lay in bed trying to go to sleep, the remembered feel of Frank's lips on hers taunted her. The realization that she wanted to trust him shook her. You are definitely treading on unsafe ground, she cautioned herself.

Chapter Seven

The next morning as she dressed for work, she dreaded facing Frank. "Act like nothing happened last night," she ordered the image in the mirror. "Play it cool." But her own duplicity tormented her. A part of her wanted Frank to obey her request while another part wanted to feel the strength of his arms around her once again. Be very careful, she warned herself.

She entered the office with an expression of cool reserve on her face. But Frank wasn't there. Instead there was a note from him on the desk. It said the driver he'd hired for the short run to Dover, Delaware had called in sick and he was taking the run himself. He also asked her to feed the dogs.

She frowned as she read the note. "He shouldn't be driving yet," she muttered aloud. Chewing on her bottom lip, she told herself that people drove with broken arms and that Frank knew what he was doing. Still she couldn't entirely forget how tired he'd looked or the pain she'd seen on his face when he used his wounded arm. She also found herself remembering his kiss. Her blood began to race and she had to admit that it was probably good that she didn't have to face him again so soon.

"Obviously I need a little more time away from him to get my emotions back under control," she told the dogs as she filled their dishes.

In unison they tilted their heads to one side and stared up at her questioningly.

"You think he's terrific, don't you?" she continued with a frown. "Well, let me tell you, he's a man and it can be very dangerous for a woman to trust one of those."

Rough and Ready continued to regard her in the same questioning manner.

"Well, it can be," she insisted firmly, setting their dishes in front of them.

Immediately the dogs lost interest in her or anything she was saying as they started to eat.

"Thanks for listening, guys," she muttered and went back to the office.

The day went well. Frank's old customers were coming back and she was able to set up a full schedule of runs.

But around five o'clock she began to feel anxious. Frank should have been back by now. She told herself that if he'd had an accident, the police would have called, but that didn't help. "He probably just had engine trouble," she reasoned as she went out to feed the dogs. "Or maybe it took longer than he expected to pick up the load he was supposed to deliver on his return trip.

"He's a big boy. He can take care of himself," she assured herself, when he still hadn't shown up by five-thirty.

She told herself to go home. Half a dozen times between five-thirty and six, she started to leave. But she couldn't. She needed to know he was safe.

Finally giving in to her nerves, she locked the gate. Going into the office, she paced. "I'll tell him I got behind on my paperwork and stayed late to catch up," she informed the dogs as they sat watching her.

Night fell and still no Frank. Her anxiety grew.

The clock struck nine. Suddenly she felt like a fool. What if he was late because he'd stopped to see a girlfriend? "At least that would cure this attraction I feel for him," she philosophized. This thought, which should have produced a feeling of relief, only caused a hard knot in her stomach.

Suddenly Rough sat up and barked. Ready let out a yelp, too, and they both stood anxiously in front of the door. Opening it for them, Laura saw a truck pulling up to the gate. It was Frank.

Quickly, she scattered a few papers over the desk to make it look as if she'd been working. Then, making certain her cool demeanor was in place, she walked out to meet him.

"Something go wrong today?" he asked worriedly, as he climbed down from the cab.

"Just got a little behind on my paperwork," she replied with cool nonchalance.

He was watching her narrowly. "If I was a suspicious man, I'd think you were waiting for me."

"Well, I wasn't," she assured him stiffly. But the anxiety that had been building for the past hours was too strong to suppress. "But you should've called. You were supposed to be back by five."

"Careful," he cautioned. "I might get the impression that you didn't mean what you said last night about my staying away from you."

She started to assure him that she had meant it but her throat constricted. Turning, she stalked into the office and grabbed her purse. But as she went to leave, Frank was blocking the doorway.

"I got caught in thunderstorms so heavy the windshield wipers couldn't keep up. Had to pull off the road several times. And I guess I was more tired than I thought. The last time I was forced to stop, I fell asleep. When I woke up, it was past seven. I figured you'd already be gone."

Again her pent-up anxiety overcame her control. "You shouldn't have taken this run, anyway," she heard herself saying. "Your arm isn't well enough."

"For someone who professes to want me to stay away from her, you sure seem awfully interested in my health and well-being," he observed dryly.

He was mocking her. An embarrassed flush darkened her cheeks. "From now on, Mr. Davidson, I promise you I won't concern myself with any of your activities," she said stiffly. "Now if you'll please get out of my way, I'll be leaving."

But he didn't move. Drawing a tired breath, he said gruffly, "I didn't mean that the way it sounded. I took the run because I needed the time away from you. I needed time to think." There was frustration in the dark depths of his eyes. Moving toward her, his hands closed around her upper arms. "Do you have any idea how crazy you make me? From the first time I saw you, you've threatened my peace of mind. I was actually jealous when I heard you flirting with Joe Monroe. I called myself crazy for feeling that way about a woman I didn't even know and one I wasn't certain I could trust. Then you insisted on inviting yourself along on the run I was planning to use to catch the thieves. You were a real distraction. I found myself wishing you were on my side."

Releasing her, he paced across the room. With several feet between them, he turned to face her as he continued gruffly, "When I carried you out of that burning room, you felt so right in my arms. When you clung to me, I wanted to keep holding you forever."

"You so much as accused me of being one of the crooks," she pointed out shakily, frantic to find some way of fighting the effect he was having on her. Looking at her the way he was, saying the things he was saying, he was seriously threatening the wall of resistance she was desperately trying to maintain, and she was scared.

"I know," he admitted, raking a hand through his hair. "I was having a hard time telling the good guys from the bad guys. But no one was more relieved than I was when Ted was proven innocent. I wanted the chance to get close to you. But you made it clear you wanted distance between us. I told myself that was fine with me. I've never liked vindictive people. But then you didn't act vindictive. When I was shot, you insisted on taking care of me. You even helped take care of my dogs. And you didn't make one sound of complaint when we got stuck with two babies." A gentleness entered his eyes. "In fact you handled them very well." The gentleness was replaced by frustration. "You had me so confused I didn't know what to think. One minute you were mothering me and the next you were telling me to keep my distance. Then last night happened."

She watched him as he strode across the office toward her. When he came to a halt in front of her, she ordered herself to back away from him. It wasn't safe with him standing so close. But her legs refused to respond.

His hands gently captured her by the upper arms as if he sensed her desire to run, and he looked hard into her face. "When I kissed you last night, it seemed so right. And I know you felt the same way, too. I could feel you responding.'' His gaze became even more intense. ''It was as if you belonged in my arms.'' The frown on his face deepened. ''Then you suddenly pulled away. I want to know why. I want to know what has made you so afraid of me.''

She tried to speak. She wanted to tell him coolly that she wasn't afraid of him. But that was a lie. The truth was that she was terrified of him. He made her feel things she had never wanted to feel.

He kissed her lightly on the forehead and then on the lips. ''I would never do anything to hurt you.''

She wanted to believe him more than she'd ever wanted to believe anyone in her life.

Releasing her arms, he cupped her face. His fingers combed into her hair as he stroked the line of her jaw with his thumbs. ''Trust me, Laura,'' he said huskily.

His mouth descended on hers, claiming it fully.

Her whole body felt as if it were going to ignite. Tremblingly, her hands traveled over his chest, upward to his shoulders. He felt so strong, so safe.

But he isn't safe! her little voice screamed. How do you know he won't betray you? Suddenly her arms stiffened and she pushed against him.

Releasing her, he looked hard into her face. ''What's wrong, Laura? Talk to me,'' he ordered gruffly.

She didn't want to talk. She just wanted out of there. She tried to get past him, but again he caught her. Holding her pinned in front of him, he studied her grimly. "You're not running away from me this time. I want to know what's going on."

"Let go of me," she demanded, finding her voice at last.

"No." His hands on her arms tightened. "I want some answers. I want the truth. You do care for me, don't you?"

"Yes, yes," she admitted through clenched teeth. Hot tears burned at the back of her eyes. "But I don't want to! I don't want to!" She had to get out of there.

She pushed against him, but he continued to hold her. "Why?" he demanded.

She faced him defiantly. "Because I won't be made a fool of."

"I'm not going to make a fool of you," he promised.

She shook her head. "I can't trust you."

"I've never done anything to you to make you think you can't trust me," he argued tersely.

Tears of frustration brimmed in her eyes. "It isn't you."

"Talk to me, Laura," he coaxed demandingly. "Tell me what I'm up against."

The scarlet blush of embarrassment flamed on her cheeks. "I can't."

"Yes, you can." His gaze burned into her, willing her to obey him. "You're not leaving here until you do."

She knew he meant it and she didn't have the will to fight him any more. Drawing a shaky breath, she lowered her gaze to the floor. "My father died twelve years ago. He had a good job, but we didn't have much. He told my mother they had to save for their future, so we were always on a very tight budget. He insisted on handling all the money and gave her a miserly allowance on which she had to manage. He was always working late and he traveled a lot. But she never complained. She trusted him implicitly. Then he died."

A cold chill shook her. She pushed against Frank again. This time he released her. Her gaze shifted absently to the papers on the desk as her mind filled with images.

"It was probably one of the most embarrassing funerals the funeral director ever conducted. These women started showing up. They had expensive clothes and jewelry and drove fancy cars. There were three in all. They turned out to be his mistresses." A bitter smile curled her lips. "While my mother, brother and I were all living from hand to mouth, he'd been spending the major portion of his money on these women. Even worse, he'd spent my mother's money on them. Her parents had left her a small inheritance and their farm just outside of Kansas City when they died. She'd turned the money over to him and since we weren't going to farm the land, he'd also talked her into selling all but a couple of acres and turning that money over to him, too. Luckily for us, the house was still in her name or we would've been out on the street. He'd left some insurance but by the time the funeral was paid for and his debts cleared, there was nothing left."

She drew a terse breath. "But the worse part was what it did to my mother. She'd loved him and trusted him and he betrayed her. She became a bitter woman who merely existed from day to day. She never laughed or cried. When she found out she had cancer, she didn't even fight it. She just let herself die."

"I am not like your father," Frank said levelly.

She turned to face him. "How do I know that?" She spread her hands in a helpless gesture. "Maybe what hurts the most is that I loved him and I trusted him, too. He could be so charming." Then licking her suddenly dry lips, she said quietly, "Now I'm the one who doesn't know how to tell the good guys from the bad guys."

"I'm one of the good guys, Laura," Frank said firmly.

She looked up into his face. "I really want to believe that," she admitted.

He dropped a light kiss on the tip of her nose. "Then I guess I'm going to have to find a way to prove it to you."

Hesitantly, she reached up and touched the hard line of his jaw. "I wish you could."

"I will," he assured her with a confident smile.

His smile was contagious and a small, wistful smile tilted the corners of her mouth.

"And now is as good a time as any to get started," he said. Slipping an arm around her waist, he guided her toward the door. "I'm going to buy you dinner and we're going to discuss how many children we're going to have."

Laura looked up at him in surprise. "You really are very sure of yourself," she mused, the thought of having his children causing a warm glow within her.

His hold on her tightened. "You're a challenge I don't intend to lose."

A sudden apprehension filled her. Maybe that was what she really was to him . . . merely a challenge. You do have a distrusting mind, she chided herself. Better to be safe than sorry, her little voice countered. But this time she ignored it. Frank's arm around her felt strong and secure, and she wanted to put the past behind her.

It was late and a week night. All the fancier restaurants had stopped serving and they ended up at the Twenty-Four Hours Café.

"You really know how to turn a girl's head," she teased him, trying to relax and let whatever was going to happen between them just . . . happen.

He laughed. "That's good. In the trucking business you need a sense of humor."

She loved the sound of his laughter. It was so open, so honest, and he was looking at her with an intensity that was causing her heart to pound erratically. "Tell me about yourself," she requested, wanting to know all there was to know.

Taking her hand in his, he massaged her palm with his thumb. "I believe in love, marriage and commitment."

Laura drew a shaky breath. His touch was sending currents of excitement along her arm, and she was having a very hard time thinking straight.

"Well, well," the waitress's jolly voice interrupted. For the night shift, the blonde had been replaced by an older woman. Laura guessed she was in her early forties. She was a little on the heavy side with red hair, green eyes and an open smile. "This is a real news item," the woman continued with a laugh. "Frank Davidson actually holding hands in public. I can hear hearts breaking all over the county."

Laura's body stiffened. You can't expect him to have never looked at another woman, she chided herself. That would be not only unfair but unreasonable. Still, she couldn't make herself relax.

"You two ready to order?" the waitress continued in the same jocular voice.

"Yeah," Frank replied, tightening his hold on Laura's hand as if he was afraid she might try to pull away. Quickly he gave the waitress their orders. The moment she was gone, his expression became serious. Leaning toward Laura, he looked intently at her. "I'm no Don Juan," he said earnestly. "Marge just likes to tease."

Laura's chin trembled. When he looked at her like that, he could make her believe anything.

Or maybe you just want to believe it so badly, you can't tell truth from fiction, she thought worriedly as she lay in bed later that night. Reva McLoyd had also alluded to the notion that there were other women interested in Frank. But he hadn't called any of them when he'd had the chance, she argued. How had he put it? He didn't want to call anyone he knew would come.

She shifted restlessly as she recalled him referring to her as a challenge. Could he be the kind of man who simply couldn't resist a challenge? Peg had dated a man like that once. The minute he was certain she'd fallen for him, he'd dropped her like a hot potato.

Laura drew a shaky breath. But Frank seemed so sincere. And from what she did know of him, he didn't seem like a man who played games.

A rush of heat spread through her as she remembered his embrace and the feel of his lips when he'd kissed her good night. He was worth the risk. "I just have to move cautiously," she ordered herself.

Chapter Eight

But moving cautiously around Frank wasn't going to be that easy, she learned the next morning. He was waiting for her. "Dave, my short-run driver, is still out with the flu," he informed her, drawing her into his arms for a good morning kiss. "I have to take the run to Atlantic City and I want you to come with me."

Laura found it exceedingly difficult to deny him anything when he was holding her so tenderly. "But who will run the office?" she questioned, trying to think rationally.

"Maryann is coming in," he replied. "I've already made the arrangements." A sudden frown came over his face. "I hope you don't mind. But I figured the only way I was going to teach you to trust me was for you to be with me as much as possible."

She felt herself getting lost in the dark depths of his eyes. "I don't mind," she assured him.

"For you, Laura, my life is going to be an open book," he promised gruffly. "There will be no secrets."

It was so easy to believe him when he was looking at her that way, she thought, feeling the cautious resistance she had tried to build during the restless night melting like butter on a hot July day. Afraid he might read in her eyes just how strong a hold he had on her, she pulled her gaze away from him. "If we don't get going, the delivery is never going to be made."

"Yes, ma'am," he replied, and after one last quick kiss, he released her.

A while later when they stopped to pick up their load, Laura sat in the truck while Frank took care of checking the invoices. She'd never thought of herself as a trucker but she felt at home in the big cab. Looking out the window, she saw Frank studying the papers on the clipboard he was holding. Just the sight of him caused a feeling of happiness to swell within her. "Your resistance to him is running practically on empty," she chided herself worriedly.

"Miss me?" he asked playfully as he climbed in behind the wheel.

"As a matter of fact, I did," she heard herself confessing.

He glanced toward her and grinned broadly. "Good."

The urge to reach over and gently touch his jaw was almost overwhelming. My resistance to him *is* running on empty, she realized, correcting her earlier assessment of the situation.

"What kind of movies do you like?" he asked unexpectedly.

"Funny ones," she answered, glad of any topic that would take her mind off of how much he was growing to mean to her.

"Do you bowl?"

"I've never tried it."

"What about pool?"

"The kind you swim in or the kind where you hit a bunch of balls around on a table with a stick?" she asked.

"The kind where you hit a bunch of balls around on a table with a stick," he replied, then grinning added, "but the other isn't a bad thought. Do you have a two-piece suit?"

The mischief in his grin caused her to laugh. "Nope."

He signed with mock regret. "Too bad. But I guess it's just as well. Keeping my hands off of you is hard enough when you're fully clothed."

Just his words sent a rush of hot excitement through her. "You are a lecherous man," she admonished with mock disapproval.

"Only where you're concerned," he assured her. Reaching over, he traced the line of her jaw with his thumb.

His touch left a trail of fire. You'll be purring in a minute, she chided herself. "Why this game of twenty questions?" she asked, trying to take her mind off the disconcerting effect he had on her.

He glanced toward her, and the warmth in his eyes could have melted an iceberg on a winter's day. "Because I want to plan things for us to do together that will make you happy."

Just being with him made her happy, but she wasn't ready to admit that to him. It frightened her to admit it to herself. These feelings she was having for him were happening much too fast. "I think it would be best if you chose things you like to do. If I'm going to learn to trust you, I need to know you better."

"All right," he agreed. "But at least give me a hint as to what you like or don't like."

"I'm not really sure," she admitted. "I never had much time just to play while my mother was alive. She required a lot of attention. After she died, I guess I just stayed in the same old rut, watching television, reading, going to a movie once in a while." A shadow flitted across her face. "It was a safe existence."

Frank glanced toward her, his jaw set in a firm line. "You are safe with me, Laura." The seriousness giving way to a mischievous grin, he added, "And I'm going to enjoy teaching you to play."

A sudden pang of anxiety shook her. I just hope this doesn't turn out to be nothing more than a game to Frank, she prayed silently.

They reached Atlantic City near noon.

While their truck was being unloaded, the foreman at the warehouse approached Frank. "If you're riding home empty and can wait around for two or three hours," he said, "an order for a shipment to Philly just came in and you can have it."

"We'll take it," Frank agreed. In the next breath, he asked if he could use the man's phone. Ten minutes later Laura found herself with Frank in a taxi heading for one of the casinos.

"I wasn't going to give you the chance to start thinking I was boring company by making you hang around a warehouse for hours," Frank said as they left the taxi and walked toward the glass doors. "We can have lunch here and then go for a walk on the boardwalk or take a look at the games."

"Boring is not a word I could easily associate with you," she replied and was rewarded with a smile that caused her heart to skip a beat.

Inside, Frank guided her along a long lobby. On one side were doors opening onto the gambling floor. On the other side were a variety of restaurants. At the far end of the room was a series of eateries providing a variety of fast foods.

Laura opted for a quick sandwich. "I'd really like to have time to see everything," she explained.

"You're the boss," Frank replied.

But while they were eating, a nagging thought suddenly brought a worried frown to Laura's face. "Do you come here often?"

Frank smiled reassuringly. "If you're asking if gambling is one of my vices, the answer is no." His expression became serious as his gaze narrowed on her with purpose. "I don't like losing."

She felt a small spasm of fear as it once again occurred to her that maybe she was simply a challenge he couldn't resist accepting. Time will tell, she told herself and again cautioned herself to go slowly. Glancing at Frank, she thought that was like telling a child not to touch a cookie that had been set right there in front of him. But you're not a child and you should be able to exercise restraint, she told herself firmly.

When they had finished eating, they wandered into the gambling room. Laura found the roulette and blackjack games interesting to watch but they didn't tempt her. However, she couldn't resist trying her luck with the slot machine.

"So down deep there does lurk the heart of a gambler," Frank teased as he handed her a roll of quarters.

"Losing a few quarters is not a dangerous gamble," she replied.

His expression became serious as he caught her chin and tilted her face upward to meet his steady gaze. "And neither am I," he assured her. "Fact is, I'm a sure bet."

She drew a shaky breath. She wanted desperately to believe that. But as he released her and she turned to put a quarter in the slot, she saw a pretty redhead standing at the end of the aisle. The woman looked to be about Laura's age and her shapely figure was well accented by a pair of tight slacks and a form-fitting sweater. She was studying Frank as if she recognized him, and Laura felt a hard knot form in her stomach. You know he's had other women friends before you came along, she chided herself again. You've got to be realistic. Aloud she said evenly, "I think a friend of yours is trying to catch your eye."

Glancing over his shoulder, Frank frowned in confusion. "Where?" he asked.

"The redhead," Laura replied, watching the woman watching Frank.

"Never seen her before," he said with a nonchalant shrug, returning his attention to Laura.

Laura saw a momentary puzzled look on the woman's face, then the redhead also gave a shrug as if to say she'd obviously made a mistake and walked away toward one of the roulette tables.

Laura felt her stomach unknot. You were so jealous it's a wonder your complexion didn't turn green, she berated herself.

Later that same evening she was forced to face an even more unsettling truth. After making the delivery to Philly, it had been late when they'd gotten to Frank's place. He'd wanted to take her out to dinner but he'd looked so tired, she'd insisted on making omelets.

"You go rest," she ordered, shooing him out of the kitchen when he offered to help. "You did all the driving. It's my turn to do the work."

A yawn interrupted his protest, and bowing to the commanding look in her eyes, he obeyed.

When the omelets were done, she went searching for him and found him asleep on the couch in the living room. She hated waking him. Kneeling down beside him, she studied the rugged lines of his face. If ever a man looked like he could be trusted, Frank Davidson was that man. Tentatively she touched his cheek. It felt rough. He needed a shave. But she liked it. In fact, she liked everything about him. You've fallen in love with him, her little voice wailed sadly. I know, she confessed. What are you going to do now? it demanded. I don't know, she answered.

Frank opened his eyes and smiled up at her. "Didn't mean to fall asleep," he apologized.

Immediately, her expression became guarded. She didn't want him to guess how totally vulnerable she was to him. "The omelets are ready," she said, rising.

He caught her hand and stopped her. "Penny for your thoughts."

"I was wondering if I should wake you," she replied.

"Not that thought." He traced the line of her jaw with the tip of his finger. "When I first opened my eyes there was a look on your face that could have melted the polar ice cap."

"Only Superman can melt the polar ice cap with a look," she bantered, refusing to make any confession she might regret later. "Now come on before the omelets get cold."

For a moment longer he hesitated, continuing to search her face. Then in a slow drawl he said, "All right, my cautious little sprite. I'll come eat your food."

During dinner, he yawned several times and she insisted on going home right after they'd finished washing the dishes. "And I will drive myself," she stipulated. "I'm afraid you might fall asleep behind the wheel. Besides, I'll need Ted's car to get to work tomorrow."

For a moment he looked as if he was going to argue but another yawn stopped him. "All right," he agreed. "But you call me the minute you get in."

"I will," she said, basking in the warm protective glow of his gaze.

Circling his arms around her, he kissed her possessively.

Later as she drove home, her mouth formed a hard straight line. You'd better be trustworthy, Mr. Frank Davidson, she thought tersely, because you're holding my heart in your hands.

The next morning she was busy organizing invoices and sorting through the mail when Frank came in.

"Come on," he ordered, flicking on the answering machine to take care of any incoming calls. Taking her by the hand, he pulled her out of her chair.

"Where are we going today?" she demanded, not really caring. The feel of his hand around hers was sending warm currents of excitement up her arm, and all she wanted was to be in his company.

"You're going to have your first lesson in how to drive a big rig," he answered, bringing her to a halt next to a cab that had been detached from its long trailer.

She looked up at him and laughed. "You can't be serious."

"Oh, yes, I am," he assured her, opening the door and motioning for her to climb up into the driver's seat. "I intend to have you participate in every aspect of my life, and that means being a driving companion on long hauls if that should ever become necessary."

She liked the idea of accompanying him on long drives but actually sitting behind the wheel was a little frightening. "I can't," she balked.

"Up!" he ordered.

Tossing him a "you'll see I'm right" look, she climbed into the driver's seat.

Going around to the other side, he climbed into the passenger's seat.

"How many gears does this thing have?" she questioned, dubiously looking at the dials and shifts around her.

"Fifteen or so," he replied.

For a moment she considered protesting again. But the truth was, now that she was in the driver's seat, it was fun sitting behind the big wheel. Tossing him a mischievous smile, she said, "If you and Ted can learn to drive one of these things, then I'm sure I can."

He grinned back. "That's the spirit."

"But first you'd better show me where the brake is," she cautioned.

"The brake was where I was going to start," he replied.

For the next two hours, he worked with her.

"It's a little confusing trying to remember everything," she said when he finally called an end to the lesson and they climbed out of the cab.

"I'm just glad you remembered where the brake was," he said, shaking his head as if he was wondering what insanity had prompted him to try teaching her to drive.

She tossed him a playfully indignant glance. "I missed hitting the tree."

Grinning crookedly, he raked a hand through his hair. "Yeah, by a full inch at least."

"By a foot," she corrected.

Stopping suddenly, he pulled her into his arms. "You're undoubtedly the cutest driver to ever scare the hell out of me."

She looked toward the cab regretfully. "I suppose this means there will be no more lessons."

He kissed her on the nose. "Nope. It just means that my nerves can't take any more today."

Laughing, she kissed him quickly on the lips. "I promise to do better tomorrow."

The brown of his eyes darkened warmly. "It was worth the terror." His gaze caressed her. "That's the first time you've ever kissed me."

She frowned up at him in confusion. "I distinctly remember kissing you before."

"I've always kissed you," he corrected. "You've never, on your very own, kissed me."

"I suppose not," she conceded. Very gently she traced the line of his jaw with the tip of her finger. She loved being in his arms. "However, I have thought about doing it several times," she said softly. Putting her words into action, she cupped his face in her hands and rising up on tiptoes, she kissed each corner of his mouth. Then very slowly she kissed him fully.

When their lips parted, he looked searchingly into her face. "Laura?"

There was a question in the dark depths of his eyes she wasn't ready to answer. "I shouldn't have done that," she said, releasing him abruptly.

"It's all right." His voice was gruff but soothing. "Don't be afraid. I know you still need time."

She looked up at him gratefully. "You really are very special."

"But I'm also only human," he reminded her. "And we'd better stop this and get back to work before my patience does begin to wear thin." Dropping a final light kiss on her forehead, he released her and gave her a push toward the office.

"Back to the nonglamorous but necessary business of running this place," she mused with playful disgruntlement.

She heard him laughing behind her and smiled. He had a really nice laugh.

That afternoon when she went to visit Ted, her brother was beaming.

"Frank called and told me you told him everything," he said. "He also said he was determined to teach you to trust him." Ted's expression became serious. "You can trust him, Laura."

"I'm beginning to believe that," she confessed. "But don't tell him that," she added. "I still need a little more time."

"My lips are sealed." He pursed them together and made a locking motion with his hands. Then taking her hand in his, he said, "I've always hated the idea that you would grow old alone and bitter because you were afraid to fall in love...afraid you might be hurt. Sometimes you have to take a risk."

She knew he was right. Still she couldn't help feeling scared. "You're a fine one to talk about taking risks," she muttered, her eyes traveling pointedly over his cast-encased body.

"Well, it got you out of that smothering cocoon you'd wrapped around yourself," he said with a grin. "And I've got the cutest nurse in Pennsylvania looking after me."

She shook her head at his logic. "You always could find the bright side to any situation."

His expression became serious once again. "It's time you started looking for the bright sides, too. It's time you started living life instead of hiding from it."

"You're right," she conceded.

That night Frank had another surprise for her. He ordered a take-home dinner, then, seating her on the couch, he produced a whole stack of albums. "I had George stop by my parents' place and pick these up on his Ohio run," he explained. "It's my life as portrayed in pictures."

For several hours, Laura looked through the albums with Frank. His whole family was there, and he told her the stories that went with some of the snapshots. Most were funny, and all of them had a warmth that demonstrated how close his family was.

"You have a very nice family," she said as they closed the last book.

"Just as nice as the one we're going to have," he replied confidently.

Lost in the warmth of his gaze, Laura believed him. "Just as nice," she heard herself saying.

A nervousness swept over her as triumph flashed in his eyes. She hadn't meant to be so open but it was hard to control her thoughts when he was so near.

"I know I promised to be patient, Laura," he said gruffly, gently stroking her cheek. "But it's not easy. I've never felt this way before. It's like I need you with me to be complete. I love you, Laura. We belong together." He gazed beseechingly into her eyes. "Marry me," he coaxed.

She knew to agree so quickly would be imprudent. She had promised herself she would proceed carefully, take her time. But when he looked at her the way he was looking now, she couldn't think rationally. "Yes," she heard herself say softly.

He let out a triumphant laugh as he pulled her into his arms. "You'll never regret this," he promised against her lips.

All doubt vanished as his mouth claimed hers fully. Every instinct told her this was where she belonged. Something that feels this right can't be wrong, she told herself.

"Two weeks," Frank said, dropping light kisses on her lips as he lifted his head from hers.

"Two weeks?" she questioned, having trouble thinking coherently with him still holding her so close.

"The wedding will take place in two weeks," he elaborated, combing a wayward strand of hair from her face and tucking it behind her ear. "I made Ted a promise that I would treat you proper and by the book. However, while I'm a patient man, I don't think I can wait more than two weeks to have you in my bed."

Laura felt a rush of excited expectation. "Two weeks," she agreed.

Chapter Nine

The next few days were hectic but Laura loved every minute. The wedding was to take place in Ted's hospital room so he could be in attendance, and all of Frank's immediate family was coming. It would be a little crowded but Laura didn't care. She just wanted to be Frank's wife.

She was humming happily one bright spring morning just eight days from the date of the wedding as she turned into the drive leading to Frank's place. All the arrangements were coming along beautifully.

But as she left her car to unlock the padlock and swing the gate open, a questioning frown replaced the smile on her face. Parked near the path leading to the house was a white sports car. Maybe one of Frank's brothers or sisters was able to come early, she decided, suddenly nervous about meeting a member of his family. Climbing into her car, she drove onto the lot. As she parked, she saw someone coming down the path from the house. It was a woman...a redhead. She was dressed in skintight white jeans and a blousy pullover sweater. Rough and Ready flanked her on both sides and she was laughing and petting them playfully as she walked.

Laura squinted to focus better. There was something very familiar about the woman. As the redhead neared the sports car, Laura's stomach knotted. It was the woman she had seen in the casino in Atlantic City...the one Frank had said he didn't know.

Spotting Laura, the woman's smile suddenly vanished.

Forcing her legs to move, Laura approached the redhead.

"Now I'm in trouble," the woman moaned unhappily. "I promised Frank I would be gone by the time you arrived."

"Who are you?" Laura demanded.

"I'm just an old friend," the woman replied with a nonchalant shrug.

"We saw you in Atlantic City," Laura said tersely, wanting to verify her recognition.

The redhead nodded. "Yeah."

"You acted as if you'd made a mistake when you thought you recognized Frank," Laura persisted, not wanting to believe the ugly thoughts going through her mind.

"Frank and I have been friends a long time. We know each other real well," the woman replied. "I could tell he didn't want me interrupting the two of you."

Laura's chin tightened. "He said he didn't know who you were."

The woman smiled brightly. "There, you see, I was right. He didn't want me interrupting."

Laura felt the bile rising in her throat. Still she wanted to trust Frank. "What exactly are you doing here?" she asked levelly.

"I can see you're upset, Laura," the woman said in soothing tones. "I hope you don't mind if I call you Laura?" She smiled self-consciously, then hurried on in a friendly tone, "You're just what Frank has always wanted...the motherly type who'll have his kids and keep his home comfortable. Me..." The redhead paused and let out a little laugh. "I'm not the least bit interested in a bunch of little brats or settling down. I cherish my freedom." A sober look came onto the redhead's face. "Please don't be angry with Frank. You can't blame him for one last little fling before he ties the knot."

Laura felt dizzy, then realized she had been holding her breath in an attempt to maintain control. Frank had lied to her. He had betrayed her! She didn't want to believe it but the proof was too strong to ignore. The woman was standing right in front of her, telling her that she'd spent the night with him. And there was the fact that the redhead had been inside the locked enclosure and the dogs were treating her like a long-time friend. "Where's Frank now?" Laura questioned, her body stiffening for a confrontation.

The redhead yawned and stretched as if she was still trying to wake up. "Oh, he had a call real early this morning about one of his trucks. Seems a driver decided he wanted to get home sooner so he drove all night. Apparently he fell asleep at the wheel and ran off the road. No one was hurt but the truck was damaged. It was about fifty miles up on the interstate so Frank took off to check it out himself." She frowned petulantly. "I should have left then, too, but it was so cozy under the covers." The redhead leaned down and gave Rough one last stroke on the head, then again turning to Laura she said, "It's been real nice meeting you. You and Frank are going to make the perfect couple."

When hell freezes over, Laura thought as she watched the white sports car going down the drive. If he would betray her eight days before the wedding, she knew he'd betray her afterward. "I wasn't born yesterday," she muttered to herself.

Going into the office, she glanced at the desk. There was a note from Frank.

Laura,

Got a call about one of the trucks. It was in an accident. No one was hurt but the truck was damaged. Have gone to check. See you this evening. Miss me a little . . . no, make that a lot.

I love you,
Frank

Hot tears burned at the back of her eyes. He had a whole different view of love than she did, she thought bitterly. As for missing him, she was never even going to think about him again!

Her hands were shaking so badly it took three attempts to punch in Maryann's number. When Maryann answered, Laura asked her to come in and work.

"Need some extra time to get the wedding arranged?" Maryann asked brightly after saying she'd be happy to come in.

Laura was tempted to tell her bluntly that there was never going to be a wedding but that would lead to a lot of questions she didn't want to answer. "There have been some unexpected last-minute developments," she replied.

"You sound a bit on edge," Maryann noted, adding in motherly tones, "Now don't go getting yourself all upset. There are always little complications that arise when you're planning a wedding. They always work themselves out."

Not this one, Laura thought as she hung up.

Finding a notepad, she scribbled a quick note to Frank. It read:

Mr. Davidson,

I may be naive but I know now that you are one of the bad guys. I'm just grateful I discovered the truth before I'd actually married you. Stay out of my life. Goodbye

Laura

Finishing, she sealed the note in an envelope, put Frank's name on the front and left it on the desk beside the note he'd left.

Then locking the gate behind her, she drove away from Frank's place. If I never see him again, I'll die happy, she told herself. The tears behind her eyes were burning hotter but she refused to allow them to escape. She wasn't going to cry over a man who could lie to her so blithely.

At Ted's apartment she called the airlines. There was a plane leaving for Kansas City in a little over two hours, and they had a seat available. She took it. She called the airport limousine service, and again luck was with her. They had a van that could pick her up in time to catch the plane. Not caring about neatness, she shoved her clothes into her suitcases. All she wanted was to get away from here as quickly as possible.

Catching a glimpse of Ted's picture on the mantel, she glanced toward the phone. She had to let him know she was leaving. Picking up the receiver, she dialed the hospital and asked for his room.

"You sound terrible, Sis," he said when he heard her voice. "You aren't coming down with the flu, are you?"

"No." It was hard talking around the lump in her throat but she was determined not to cry. "I just wanted you to know that I'm going home. The wedding is canceled."

"What happened?" he demanded protectively.

In her mind's eye, Laura again saw the redhead, but when she tried to tell Ted about the woman, the words refused to come. The pain was too great. "I can't talk about it now," she replied, fighting to keep the catch out of her voice. "I just have to go." Hanging up, she picked up her bags, carried them outside and waited for the limo. She could hear the phone ringing inside but she didn't dare answer it. She knew it was Ted and she was afraid if she heard his voice again, she would burst into tears.

All during the ride to the airport, the flight to Kansas City and the ride to her farm, she held herself under tight control.

Unlocking her front door, she went inside. A chill shook her and, switching on the lights, she found the thermostat and turned up the heat. Still a coldness filled her. As her gaze traveled over the familiar furnishings, her jaw tensed. The house didn't feel safe any longer, it felt more like a prison. Leaving her suitcases by the door, she sank down into one of the overstuffed chairs in the living room.

At least her experience with Frank hadn't been totally wasted, she told herself philosophically as her gaze continued to travel over the pictures and the furniture. She'd learned a lot about herself. She wasn't her mother. Just because she'd been hurt she had no desire to crawl away into some hole and die. Tomorrow, she'd go looking for a job. And she'd put this place up for sale. She'd find an apartment in town and she'd start dating. She knew now that she didn't want to live her life alone. She wanted a husband and a family. "But next time I will go more slowly and be much more careful," she promised herself.

The phone rang. Assuming it was Ted calling to make certain she had arrived safely, she rose and, crossing to the hall table, answered it.

"Laura?" It was Frank's voice on the other end. He sounded worried and confused. "What the devil..."

The knuckles of the hand holding the phone turned white as she fought for control. A bitter smile curled her lips. He sounded so sincere! But she wasn't going to be taken in by his tricks again. Refusing to dignify his call with a response, she dropped the receiver back into place before he'd even finished.

She was on her way to pick up her suitcases and carry them upstairs when it rang again. Stiffly returning to the phone, she picked up the receiver, then without even putting it to her ear, she dropped it back into the cradle.

Before Frank could dial again, she called Ted. "I'm home," she informed him tightly.

"What happened?" he demanded again. "Frank called me. He swears he didn't do anything that could upset you and send you running for cover."

"He's a very good liar," Laura replied. "And I'm not running for cover. I've learned that I'm tougher than I thought. I'm not going to hide from the world.

I'm going to start really living life. I just don't ever want to see Frank Davidson again."

"Laura, talk to me," Ted pleaded. "Tell me what happened."

Laura drew a deep breath. In her mind's eye she saw the redhead walking down the path from Frank's house with his dogs. But when she tried to tell Ted, the words caught in her throat. "I can't talk about it just yet," she said with a catch. "I'll call you tomorrow." Before he could protest, she pressed her finger on the button and disconnected them. Then, leaving the receiver off the hook, she carried her suitcases upstairs.

Like a woman with a purpose, she set her suitcases down in her bedroom, then went downstairs. First she called the Howards to let them know she was back. They had been watching over the house for her. Even though they lived a fair distance down the road, they were sure to notice her lights after dark. They would come by to check on who was in the house and she was in no mood for company.

Next, she went to the grocery. There, moving with crisp, businesslike precision, she bought food and a newspaper.

Going home, she made herself a sandwich. Munching on it, she carefully went over all the help-wanted ads. She could hear the phone bleeping at her, warning her it was off the hook, but she ignored it.

Suddenly the nervous, angry energy that had carried her through the day ended abruptly. The paper blurred in front of her eyes, and the sandwich felt like a rock in her stomach. Feeling totally drained, she dragged herself upstairs, took a warm shower, then climbed into bed.

But as she lay in the dark, her blanket pulled up to her chin, a tear escaped. Against her will, it was followed by a second, then a steady stream began to run down her cheeks. A good cry isn't a weakness, she told herself, it's a catharsis, and that's just what I need. By tomorrow I'll have washed Frank Davidson out of my system once and for all. Bowing to a need too strong to resist, she allowed the tears to flow freely.

The sound of loud pounding woke Laura. Groggily she opened her eyes. They hurt and, remembering how she'd sobbed herself to sleep, she guessed they were red and swollen. Focusing on the window, she could see the night sky through the lace curtains. The pounding registered more fully, and she realized that someone was banging on the front door. Lifting her head she read the luminous dial on the clock. It was one o'clock.

"Laura, open this door!" a man's voice demanded.

Her whole body went rigid. It was Frank.

Climbing out of bed, she went over to the window. Shoving the curtains aside, she raised the window and looked down. Her room was located on the front side of the house but the porch roof obstructed her view of Frank. "Go away!" she ordered, then slammed the window shut and went back to bed.

She could hear his booted feet as he stalked off the porch and down the short flight of stairs to the walk. Then the sound stopped. "Laura, you come down here and open this door," he shouted angrily up at her window. "One way or another you're going to talk to me!"

Again tossing her covers aside, she left the bed and strode to the window. Opening it, she looked out at him. She couldn't see his face, only his shadowed outline silhouetted by the moon. She remembered how safe she had felt in his arms, and a cold chill shook her. He had deceived her very well. "You and I don't have anything to talk about," she informed him icily.

"I, at least, deserve an explanation," he argued curtly.

"You don't deserve anything!" she snapped. "I'm just glad I learned the truth about you before I made the mistake of marrying you."

"And what truth was that?" he demanded, the anger growing stronger in his voice with each word.

Laura glared down at the shadowed figure. He didn't have any right to be angry with her. She was the one who had been betrayed. "Your girlfriend left a little too late," she informed him with haughty dignity.

Frank stood with his hands on his hips, looking up at her. "What are you talking about?" he questioned in confused tones.

"The redhead in the white sports car," she hissed, furious that he would continue to try to play the innocent. "The one you didn't recognize in Atlantic City but who found her way into your bed last night." A fresh flood of angry tears threatened. Determined that he wouldn't see her cry, she again slammed the window shut.

From outside she heard his footsteps again approaching the front door. Again he pounded on the wooden barrier. "Open up, Laura!" he ordered angrily. "I'm not leaving until you tell me what the devil you're talking about!"

Striding out into the hall, she glared down at the door. How could he dare deny what she'd seen! Furious with his innocent act, she went into her room, switched on the light and grabbed her robe. She'd face him and tell him exactly what she thought of him! Glancing at herself in the mirror, she raked a hand through her disheveled hair. She looked a fright. She reached for the brush but stopped herself. What did she care what she looked like in front of Frank Davidson? She certainly wasn't interested in impressing him. Belting her robe securely, she stomped down the stairs.

But as she reached for the knob, her hand froze in midmotion. What if she broke down in front of him and made an even greater fool of herself? Then, scowling at this sudden bout of cowardliness, she forced her hand to continue and unlocked the door. Flinging it open, she faced him with self-righteous fury.

Entering, he caught her by the arm. "Now you tell me all about this redhead."

"That innocent act isn't going to work," she snapped, trying to pull free. "I trusted you once." Her voice shook as she added, "I loved you." Then her jaw hardened. "But you betrayed me."

Refusing to allow her to escape, his hold on her tightened. "Tell me about the redhead," he demanded grimly.

Giving up her struggle, she stood rigid in front of him. "All right, I'll play your little game," she said dryly. "This morning when I arrived at work, I discovered her coming down the path from your house. She made it clear she was an old and very close friend. I remembered that you'd said you didn't recognize her when we saw her in Atlantic City, but she explained that she knew you well enough to read your expression and knew you didn't want her approaching us, so she'd just walked away. Then she told me how she wasn't the marrying type and that she thought you and I would make the perfect couple. She thinks I'd make a great little wife for you and mother for your children." Venom entered Laura's voice. "She told me I shouldn't get upset because you wanted one last little fling before we were married. But I'm not stupid. If you couldn't be faithful to me now, you'd never be faithful to me after the marriage." Again she struggled to be free.

"And you believed her?" he growled.

She faced him defiantly. "She and her car were inside the enclosure, and it was locked. On top of that, your dogs treated her like a well-known friend." She jerked on her arm. "Now let go of me!"

This time he did release her. Standing like a mountain in front of her, he studied her grimly. "This morning I got a call from a woman claiming that one of my trucks had been in an accident. She wasn't totally coherent. When I got to where the accident was supposed to have taken place, there was nothing there. When I got back to my place, you were gone."

Laura wanted to believe him, but the vision of the redhead strolling casually down the path from his house with his dogs playfully flanking her was too vivid to deny. "If you didn't let her in, then how did she get inside the enclosure?" she challenged. "And if you have no idea who she is, why did Rough and Ready treat her like an old friend?"

"I suppose she could have picked the lock on the chain," he replied. "But I can't explain the dogs' behavior." His gaze locked on her. "But I didn't spend the night with a redhead or any other woman."

Laura found herself desperately wanting to believe him. He could look so sincere! Suddenly afraid of playing the part of a complete fool, she pointed toward the door. "Get out of my house and stay out of my life!" she ordered. The hot tears again began to burn behind her eyes. Terrified they might escape in front of him, she moved toward the stairs. "You can see yourself out," she ordered over her shoulder.

"Yeah," he growled. But he didn't move. Instead he continued to watch her.

Laura could feel his eyes on her all the way up the stairs, but she didn't look back. In spite of all the proof she had against him, she wanted to run into his arms. You've no pride at all, she cursed herself. Going into her bedroom, she stood by the bed, her hands balled into fists as she waited to hear him leave.

For a long moment she heard nothing, then his booted footsteps started across the hardwood floor but instead of heading for the door they came up the stairs. She spun around as he appeared in her doorway.

"You're coming back with me," he said in a voice that held no compromise.

Her eyes rounded in shock. "I am not!"

"Yes, you are." Walking over to her suitcases, he opened them. She hadn't unpacked yet and the haphazard array of clothing was still inside. Nodding with grim satisfaction, he snapped them shut. "Saves me the trouble of packing for you," he muttered, picking up the suitcases. As he headed for the door, he glanced toward her. "Get dressed," he ordered.

She watched him leave in shocked silence. Hearing the front door open and close, she ran to the window and saw him carry her bags to a car and toss them into the trunk. "He can't do this!" she hissed. She couldn't go back with him. She didn't trust herself not to give in to him.

She was halfway down the stairs when he returned to the house. "I told you to get dressed," he growled.

"I am not going with you," she said firmly.

Tossing her over his shoulder, he carried her to her bedroom.

"Put me down!" she insisted, squirming to gain her freedom.

Dropping her unceremoniously on her bed, he stood watching her grimly. Cynicism mingled with the anger in his voice. "I once had visions of you defending me with the same faith you have in Ted. Obviously your feelings for me are not as strong as they are for him. I tried the best I knew how to teach you to trust me." A bitter smile curled his lips. "But you didn't even stick around to hear my side. You immediately believed the worst of me." The grimness returned to his features. "I fully accept the fact that we are finished, that there is no future for us. But I don't like pranksters playing havoc with my life, and I intend to find out who was behind this little charade with the redhead. For that I need a bit of bait. You're it. You're coming with me, and we're going to pretend that everything is just fine between us and see what happens next. Once I know for certain who the culprit is, you're free to go lead whatever life you choose. Now get dressed or I'll dress you myself." Stalking out of the room, he slammed the door closed behind him.

For a long moment Laura lay still on the bed as the impact of Frank's words fully sank in. She did not doubt that he was telling her the truth. He honestly didn't know who the redhead was. She realized that now. But now was too late. Frank had said they were finished, that there was no future for them, and he'd meant it.

A sharp knock sounded on the door. "Get dressed," came a gruff order from the other side.

There was only anger in the voice. Rising, Laura began to put her clothes on.

Chapter Ten

During the drive to the airport, while Frank checked in the rental car, bought the airplane tickets and checked their luggage, he only spoke to Laura when it was absolutely necessary. Once they were on the plane, he immediately went to sleep.

You really blew it this time, she chided herself curtly. Even in sleep there was an angry frown on his face. But finding the redhead at his place had been a shock, she defended herself. Still, that didn't help the sinking feeling in the pit of her stomach as Frank's words echoed through her mind. He was right. She should have at least faced him.

During the ride from Philadelphia to Chadds Ford, Laura could stand the silence no longer. "Do you have any idea who might have put the redhead up to that act?"

He glanced toward her and raised a cynical eyebrow. "So you've decided to believe me?"

"It would be real stupid of you to drag me back here otherwise," she replied tiredly.

"Yeah, it would," he agreed, leaving no doubt that his only interest in her was to find the redhead.

At Ted's apartment, he carried her suitcases in and set them in the living room. "We'll need to present a pretty high profile," he said briskly. "I'll pick you up for dinner around six, then we'll go dancing."

Before she could even respond, he strode out of the room and left the apartment.

Standing there alone, Laura felt as if the walls were closing in on her. After taking a shower, she changed into some fresh clothes and went to visit Ted.

"Well, what are you going to do now?" he asked, when she finished telling him the story of what had happened.

It was the same question Laura had been asking herself for the past several hours. Her mouth formed a determined line. "Try to win him back."

Ted smiled with approval. "That's the spirit!"

"The problem is, it's easier said than done," she replied worriedly. "He's more than angry with me; he's disillusioned." Pausing, she swallowed down the large lump that had formed in her throat. "And he has a right to be," she admitted. "I never even gave him a chance to explain."

"You'll think of a way," Ted said with confidence.

Later, as she dressed for her "date" with Frank, Laura wished she had Ted's confidence. She wanted to look her best, but everything seemed to be working against her. Her makeup refused to look right. She tried on several dresses, but they all were suddenly hanging wrong. And then there was her hair. It absolutely refused to remain in any style. Finally she settled for plaiting it into a French pigtail.

By the time Frank arrived, she was a nervous wreck.

He was wearing a suit and tie, and she thought she'd never seen a man look so good. But then he looked good to her in a pair of old jeans and a shirt. "You look very handsome tonight," she said with what she hoped was a coquettish smile.

"You look nice yourself," he replied with formal politeness.

She felt the barrier between them as if it were a solid wall. Winning him back was going to be a monumental challenge, she thought worriedly.

"We'd better get going." It was an order. Frank's manner was that of a man with a purpose, but that purpose only included her as bait.

He had chosen one of the local inns with a rustic early-American atmosphere and a high-priced menu. The waiters and waitresses were dressed in early-American styles, and there was a general calm, a dignity, about the surroundings. It was the kind of place a man would take a woman to impress her. But it isn't me he's trying to snare, Laura thought sadly. However, I'm with him, and as long as we're in one another's company, I've got time to come up with some plan to prove to him that we can have a life together.

During their drive to the inn, Frank hadn't spoken to her. However, as soon as they arrived he had begun to make inconsequential conversation about the weather and the decor of the inn. He was smiling, too, and from a distance, Laura knew, it looked like a warm smile. But she was close enough to see that the warmth didn't reach his eyes.

At first she smiled back openly, hoping to break through the barrier he was determined to keep between them. But when his gaze remained cool, pride stiffened her back and her smile became guarded. Their table was beside a large window that looked out onto a small courtyard where spring flowers were in full bloom. Looking past him, she concentrated on the blooms and tried to tell herself the situation wasn't totally helpless.

Frank's small talk ran out soon after their order was taken. Unable to endure the uncomfortable silence that fell between them, Laura fought to think of something to say, something that would be clever, something that would be just right, something that would put a dent in the wall he had constructed between them. But she couldn't think of anything to fit those qualifications. Finally she settled for asking, "How was your day?"

"Busy," he replied. "How was yours?"

"Miserable" was the word that came to mind, but pride refused to allow it to be said. "Busy, too," she replied. "I went to see Ted. He's doing very well. The doctors say he'll have to stay in the hospital for a few more weeks, though."

"Sorry to hear that," Frank said with honesty. Then again the cool smile curled his lips. "But he probably won't mind that much with that pretty blond nurse giving him all that special attention."

Laura felt a twist in her stomach. It was jealousy, and that was what had gotten her into this mess in the first place, she reprimanded herself. Frank had simply been stating a truth. Carol *was* very pretty. "I suppose not," she replied levelly.

To her relief, their food began to arrive. For the rest of dinner she concentrated on eating and making small talk about the meal. The food was delicious, but Laura hardly noticed as she tried to think of some way to win Frank back. As she glanced at him surreptitiously, the sinking sensation in her stomach became even stronger. He looked determined, and a feeling of hopelessness threatened to overwhelm her. Trying not to think of the futility of her situation, she covertly examined the other diners. The redhead wasn't among them.

To her relief they did not linger over their dessert and coffee.

"We've got some dancing to do," Frank informed her as he signaled the waiter to bring the check.

The place he had chosen for their next public appearance was a country and western bar with a live band.

At least we won't have to make stilted conversation, Laura thought as they seated themselves at a table near the dance floor. The band was too loud to easily talk above.

Several of the patrons greeted Frank with a wave and friendly hello, and Laura recognized a couple of the drivers who worked for Frank. "I suppose you come here fairly often," she heard herself saying, then wished she'd bitten her tongue. She'd promised herself she wouldn't say anything that sounded like prying.

"Not too often," he replied, returning a wave from a pretty brunette across the room.

Laura's smile felt brittle. He's a free man. He has a right to flirt with whomever he wishes, she told herself. Still it hurt.

A blonde from a nearby table waved, and Frank returned that wave along with a smile. Then another brunette yelled a hello, and again Frank responded warmly.

Laura told herself to keep her mouth shut, but her nerves were on too sharp an edge. "No one is going to believe our reconciliation if you flirt with every pretty woman in the place," she heard herself remarking dryly.

Frank rewarded this observation with a cool smile. "Those are all wives of friends of mine," he said. "It would be rude for me to ignore them."

Laura wished she could just find a dark hole to crawl into. She seemed to have developed a real knack for doing and saying the wrong thing where Frank was concerned.

The band began to play a slow song, and he rose. "Maybe we should dance," he said. It was an order rather than a suggestion.

As they joined the other couples on the dance floor, she noticed that the majority of them were dancing very close. Frank drew her into an embrace that let her know that he intended for them to dance just as close. Resting her head against his chin, she followed his lead as they moved slowly to the plaintive melody. Being in his arms was bittersweet torture. As her body moved against his, every inch of her was aware of the contact. Beneath the palm of her free hand, she could feel the strong, firm muscles of his back. Her other hand, held in his grasp, was warmed by his touch.

Giving in to her desire to be close to him even if it was only for a moment, she relaxed and let her body mold to his. Immediately she felt him stiffen. "Maybe dancing wasn't such a good idea," he said gruffly, releasing her and leading her off the dance floor.

Looking up at him, she caught a glimpse of desire in his eyes before they once again became frosty. Obviously he still held some feelings for her, but equally obviously he was determined to bury them. However, if they are still there, then there is hope for us yet, she reasoned.

About half an hour later, Frank suggested they leave. Driving out of the parking lot, he said, "I didn't see your redhead, but if she shows up she's bound to hear that we are still together."

Laura nodded, wishing that were really the case. Frank's resistance to her had seemed even more determined after their one trip to the dance floor. But she wasn't ready to give up.

As they drove toward Ted's place, a question that had been nagging at her grew stronger. "What if the redhead doesn't show up again ever?" she asked hesitantly. "What if it was just someone's idea of a sick practical joke, and now they don't want to play anymore?"

"We'll give them a few days to try something else. If nothing happens, then you're free to leave," he replied coldly.

And good riddance, Laura added to herself, watching the hard line of his jaw. "What about the wedding?" she questioned stiffly.

He glanced toward her with a cynically raised eyebrow. "What about it?"

Pride caused her back to straighten. He had a right to be angry, but he didn't have to treat the mere mention of their wedding with such total disdain. "I know you have no intention of going through with it, but if we just cancel it, this plan won't work," she pointed out with level dignity. "We need some reason to postpone it."

"We'll say that some of the members of my family couldn't make it here as quickly as we had hoped, so we've decided to reschedule it for a time when everyone can come and share our happy moment," he replied sarcastically.

"Fine," she agreed tightly. She tried reminding herself of the glimpse of passion she'd seen in his eyes, but that didn't help against the icy chill that filled the car.

By the time they arrived at Ted's apartment, Laura's nerves were on a razor's edge.

"You'd better ask me in for a minute," Frank directed.

Laura glanced at him, shocked that he wanted to spend even one more second with her. Then it dawned on her that if someone was watching them, she and Frank would be expected to exchange a good-night kiss at her door, and he was looking for a way to avoid that. Unlocking the door, she stepped inside and waited for him to enter.

When he did come in, he only came far enough to allow himself to close the door. Then, leaning against it, he checked his watch. "I'll just wait ten minutes," he said. "That should be long enough for a proper goodbye as far as anyone keeping an eye on our movements would be concerned."

Laura stood a few feet away. Her hopes for a reconciliation were growing slimmer by the moment. Still she could not just give up. "Would it make any difference," she asked levelly, "if I admitted that I was wrong? That I shouldn't have run? That I should have stayed and confronted you? That I should have given you a chance to deny the woman's accusations?"

Straightening away from the door, a grimness etched itself into his features. "That's this time. What about the next time something happens that challenges your trust in me, Laura?" His jaw hardened. "I don't want a wife I have to keep chasing after and dragging home." Then as if he found her company too unpleasant to endure for any longer, he left.

Staring at the closed door, she felt helpless. There was no way to prove she would trust him in the future. All she could do was tell him she would, and he was in no mood to listen or believe. A bitter tear rolled down her cheek.

The next morning she awoke with a throbbing headache. She had half a mind to call Frank and tell him she wasn't coming in to work, but pride made her decide against that course of action. She wasn't going to let him think she couldn't face him. He was the one who was being stubborn and bullheaded. He was the one, she added with a slight tremble of her chin, who didn't love her enough to want to work out this trouble between them.

He was inspecting the engine of a truck when she drove onto the lot. Acknowledging her presence with a wave, he rubbed his hands off on a rag as he climbed down from the ladder and walked toward her.

She waited beside the office door, a part of her hoping he might have changed his mind during the night. But the coldness was still in his eyes as he reached her.

"Morning," he greeted her, kissing her lightly on the lips.

She knew it was all for show and she was determined not to feel anything. But her traitorous body refused to obey. The warmth of his lips lingered tauntingly on hers. Angrily she reached up and brushed her hand across her mouth as soon as she was in the office and away from the view of anyone watching from outside.

But Frank had followed her inside and saw it. She caught the cynical look he tossed her and she gave him a cold glance in return. He hadn't wanted to kiss her so why should he care if she didn't want the feel of it lingering on her?

"I've got a motor that needs overhauling," he said. "I'll be out in the yard if you need me."

"I don't expect to need you for anything," she replied tightly, seating herself behind the desk and pulling out the schedule.

"That's just fine by me," he growled over his shoulder as he turned and walked out of the office.

The morning passed like a year for Laura. Every time she looked out the window she saw Frank, and as hard as she tried not to feel anything, anger and frustration filled her. Even worse, there was that dull ache that no amount of pride could make go away.

Around noon, he entered the office. "Come on," he ordered.

Remaining seated she stared up at him icily. "Where to?"

"Up to the house," he replied. "If someone is watching, they'll expect us to eat together."

Laura balked. She just couldn't sit across a table from him. She knew he'd watch her in a stony silence while she forced herself to eat so he wouldn't know how much he was hurting her. Her nerves wouldn't take it, and she had no intention of making herself look like a fool yet again. "They'll just have to assume I had too much work to do to join you," she replied.

For a long moment he regarded her in silence, then he turned and walked toward the door. "Suit yourself," he said as he left.

She didn't see him again until around two when she was getting ready to go visit Ted. As she left the office, Frank again left the engine he was working on and approached her.

Catching up with her as she reached Ted's car, he said, "I'll be by to pick you up at six for dinner."

"No," she said firmly. There was no way in the world she could keep up the charade between them for a public display. "I'll pick up a couple of carry-out dinners and bring them back here. That way you can keep working on your truck and I can read a book. *And* we can stay out of one another's way."

"Yeah," he agreed as if he, too, wasn't looking forward to another evening of feigning a loving relationship.

Again he dropped a light kiss on her lips and again, in spite of her determination to feel nothing, a lingering warmth remained.

"From the look on your face, I'd say things aren't going too well," Ted said as she entered his room a little while later.

Laura frowned. "I thought I was putting on a better show than that."

"I'm your brother, I know what it means when you get that look in your eye," he replied. He patted the side of the bed. "Come tell old Ted all about it."

As she seated herself in a chair instead, the frown on her face deepened. "It's just not going to work out for Frank and me," she said bluntly.

"Are you sure?" he asked studying her worriedly.

"Positive," she replied, feeling more certain than ever that Frank had never really loved her. But she wasn't ready to confess that even to Ted. "Now how about a game of gin rummy?" she asked, determined to change the subject.

"I could have sworn the two of you were perfect for one another," Ted persisted.

Me, too, Laura thought, then scowled at herself. Aloud, she said grimly, "It hasn't been a total loss. I have learned a valuable lesson from all this. The next time I think something is too good to be true, I'll know it is." Then, her mouth forming a hard, straight line to signal that she considered this conversation ended, she shuffled and dealt the cards.

Back at Frank's place, Laura found him still working on the truck.

"I'll put your dinner in the oven," she called out, and quickly headed toward the house. She was in no mood for one of his impersonal little kisses.

But as she neared the porch, she heard a car pulling in. Glancing over her shoulder, she froze in midstride. It was the white sports car with the redhead behind the wheel.

Laura watched in stunned silence as the woman parked next to Ted's car and climbed out. She had never expected the redhead to simply drive in and face her and Frank. She glanced toward Frank and saw her own surprise mirrored on his face. But as he started toward the white car, the surprise was replaced by anger.

Laura reached the redhead in the same instant as Frank.

There was fear in the woman's eyes, and a look of honest remorse on her face. Facing Frank levelly, she said, "I've come here to apologize."

His gaze narrowed on her, and the scowl on his face deepened. "There is something very familiar about you," he growled. "I just can't place it."

She nodded. "I'm Connie Kyle, Bill's wife. When you knew me before I was a blonde and wore a lot more makeup. I've had a nose job, too."

"You liked the dogs and felt sorry for them because they had to be penned up all day," he continued as if putting together pieces of the puzzle that had eluded him. "I let you feed them a couple of times. That's why they were so friendly toward you."

Connie nodded again. "When I first started watching you, they remembered me right away. They even accepted a few treats I brought them."

Frank's gaze shifted in the direction of the dogs' pen, and he shook his head. "Apparently they never forget a hand that I let feed them." Turning his gaze to Connie, he regarded her grimly. "Why did you pull that stunt on Laura?"

The redhead flushed self-consciously. "I didn't want to," she said defensively. "Bill made me do it. He can be real intimidating, even behind bars. Besides, I wanted a divorce. He's not exactly the greatest guy in the world to be married to. Anyway, he said he'd give it to me if I'd cause you some trouble. But afterward, I felt real bad." She looked at Frank with apology in her eyes. "You were always real nice to me." Then drawing a deep breath, she continued. "Anyway I went to see Bill right away and told him I'd done what he wanted and now he had to give me my divorce. But he just laughed and said I had to keep causing trouble until he decided I'd done enough. Well, I just couldn't, so I went to see this lawyer and he said I didn't need Bill's consent for the divorce. Anyway, this morning I went back to see Bill and told him I was getting the divorce whether he liked it or not and I wasn't going to cause you any more trouble. Well, he flew into a rage. I've seen him angry, but I've never seen him that angry. I was real glad there were bars between him and me. He was yelling and screaming, and the guard was trying to get hold of him, then Bill suddenly clutches his chest and collapses. Next thing I know the doctor's pronouncing him dead of a heart attack and I'm feeling safe for the first time in years. Then I got to thinking about the two of you. I didn't like what I'd done and with Bill dead and no threat to me if I tried to undo the damage, I decided I should come back here and try to make amends." Connie smiled nervously. "I'm real glad to find the two of you still together and that there was no permanent damage done."

"Right," Frank muttered.

Obviously unnerved by the continued anger on Frank's face, Connie eased herself into her car. "I wish you both the best," she yelled out the window as she started the engine and put the car into reverse.

Laura stood watching the white sports car as it sped down the drive. It was over. This time it was all really over. Bill Kyle was dead, her brother was a free man, and she and Frank would be going their separate ways.

Chapter Eleven

"I really want to hate her," Frank said grimly, breaking the silence between him and Laura as the white sports car pulled out onto the main road and disappeared from their view. "But I suppose I should be grateful to her. She saved me from discovering too late that I had married a woman who didn't love me enough to even want to try to trust me."

Laura turned to glare at him. He wasn't going to place the blame for all that happened between them on her shoulders. "You know what I think," she said curtly. "I think you never loved me, not really, not ever." Tears of anger burned at the back of her eyes. "I think I was only a challenge to you. I think you're glad all this happened because it gave you an excuse to get rid of me. I think once you'd made me fall in love with you, you got tired of me." Suddenly a whiff of wind carried the aroma of the bag of food she was still holding to her nostrils. It was Chinese food! She'd bought Chinese food. She hadn't thought about it when she bought it. She'd simply stopped at the most convenient place on her way back. Now she remembered that they'd had the same meal the night he'd proposed. Without even thinking about what she was doing, she reached inside the bag. The container of sweet and sour pork was on top. It was only lukewarm now, and the lid popped open with no effort. She knew she wasn't thinking rationally, but she didn't even try to stop herself as she pulled out the container and emptied it on his head.

Frank cursed as the sauce drizzled down his face.

Too furious to even feel shocked by what she'd done, Laura said with musing dryness, "Sweet and sour sauce does seem to suit you perfectly."

Raking a hand through his hair to rid it of lingering pieces of food, Frank glared down at her.

"You think I was playing some sort of game?" he demanded angrily. "You think I spent all those restless hours trying to come up with ways to make you trust me just to satisfy my male ego?" His jaw hardened. "I went half crazy when I got back here and found your note. I chased you halfway across this country just to find out what had happened." He cupped her face in his hands. "I loved you, Laura. I still do," he added in a voice that made it sound like a curse. "But I can't live my life with a woman who is going to run at the first sign of trouble. I want a wife who'll stand by me, who'll believe in me no matter what happens." Releasing her abruptly, he strode toward the house.

Laura stood rigid watching his departing back. He loved her!

Her face felt sticky and reaching up, she realized he had left sweet and sour sauce where his hands had held her. An embarrassed flush reddened her cheeks as she recalled the food running down his face. "That was a mistake," she muttered with self-directed recrimination. But a minor one compared to the others she'd made.

As the front door of his house slammed shut with a loud bang, signaling his determination to keep her out of his life, her jaw hardened with equal determination. She'd find a way to change his mind!

Setting the bag of food on the hood of Ted's car, she found a napkin and wiped off her chin and neck. It wasn't going to be easy. He was really angry with her and she knew from experience that he could be extremely bullheaded. But he was worth fighting for.

Darkness was settling in and the pole lights on the lot switched on. Walking down to the gate, she pulled it closed and locked it. Next she fed the dogs and let them out. Then returning to Ted's car, she climbed up onto the hood and sat cross-legged, Indian fashion, staring toward the house. There had to be a way to convince him she belonged in his life. The problem was finding it.

The dogs found the remains of the sweet and sour pork and ate it.

"You two are certainly not very astute guard dogs," she chided them. They looked up at her as if she didn't know what she was talking about, then took off at a run after some animal whose scent they'd sniffed on the air.

Frank came out a while later. His hair was damp and he had on a fresh shirt and clean pair of faded jeans. Coming to a halt about five feet from the car, he stood watching her guardedly. "I think I'd better warn you," he said grimly. "If you're planning another food fight, this time I plan to retaliate."

Laura had completely forgotten about the bag of food beside her. Flushing, she shook her head. "No more food fights," she promised.

"You planning to sit out here all night?" he asked.

"Don't know," she answered hesitantly.

Frank hooked his thumbs through belt loops on his jeans. "You got something on your mind you want to talk to me about or are you just enjoying the night air?"

"I do have a few things I'd like to say," she replied, shocked by how calm she sounded when her whole future hung in the balance. She paused, trying to decide how best to proceed.

"Go on," he ordered gruffly, when her pause threatened to lengthen into a silence.

"I've decided that in spite of your bullheadedness, you're worth fighting for," she began stiffly. "And

I've been trying to think of a way to convince you that I can be the kind of wife you want. I just haven't been able to think of one yet." A nervous sweat broke out on the palms of her hands and she wiped them off on her slacks.

"So in spite of my faults, you've decided you still want me," he said dryly.

"That's about it," she replied. "I can't promise you that I'll be perfect. But I can promise you that I'll always be on your side." Her eyes searched his face for any sign that she might have a chance.

"I've been wondering all day if you'd decided to give up on me... if you'd decided that I wasn't worth fighting for," he said gruffly. "I'd decided that you had, and it was tearing me apart."

She stared at him incredulously. "You've been wondering if I was going to fight for you?"

He studied her levelly. "I figured if you didn't love me enough to be willing to put up the same sort of battle for me that I put up for you, we sure wouldn't be able to make it through a lifetime together."

Sliding down from the hood of the car, she stood with her hands on her hips and glared at him. "Do you have any idea what you've put me through these past couple of days?"

"It couldn't have been any worse than the hell I've been through," he countered. "When we were dancing, you felt so good in my arms. It took every ounce of strength I had not to tell you I wanted you back on any terms you chose."

The brown of his eyes no longer held a chill, and he was looking at her in a way that was making her heart pound wildly. "I do love you, Frank Davidson," she said, adding firmly, "and I'll make you the very best wife any woman could."

Reaching her in two quick strides, he drew her into his arms as his mouth found hers for a hungry, possessive kiss.

Laura wanted to laugh and cry at the same time. Being in his arms felt so right. She knew without a doubt that she was exactly where she belonged.

"Tell me," Frank said, as he slowly lightened the contact with several smaller kisses. "If I had been more difficult to convince, did you have an alternative plan?"

"I was going to try my feminine wiles," she replied, luxuriating in the feel of him as she moved her hands slowly over his shoulders and to the strong cords at the back of his neck. "I've never had a chance to practice them but as a last hope, I figured they'd have to do."

He grinned and mischief danced in the warm depths of his eyes. "And just how did you plan to proceed?"

Playfully, she traced the line of his jaw with her fingertip. "Well, first I was going to tell you how ruggedly handsome you are and how it was only natural for me to be jealous." She kissed the hollow of his neck, then trailed kisses upward to his mouth.

"That's working very well so far," he said huskily, drawing her even closer in his arms.

"And I was going to point out that you wouldn't want a wife who took you for granted," she continued, her lips moving against his skin as she spoke.

"Agreed," he conceded, capturing her lips for another long, sweet kiss.

Lifting her head slowly away from his, her expression became serious. "One week," she said firmly.

He frowned in confusion. "One week?"

"Normally I'm a patient woman but I have no patience where you are concerned," she elaborated. The confusion on his face faded and the warmth in his eyes grew hotter. "A week is as long as I can wait for this wedding."

His hands moved with possessive intimacy along the curves of her body. "A week is too long."

She felt as if she was going to ignite under his touch. "You're right," she breathed against his lips. "I don't know what insanity made me say a week. That's seven whole days."

"I have our license up at the house," he said, teasing the taut cord of her neck with kisses.

"Do you think we could find a minister to marry us tonight?" she asked, barely able to think beyond the feel of him.

"I know I can," he promised.

Laura woke the next morning snuggled against Frank. The memories of his lovemaking brought a soft smile to her lips.

She kissed him lightly on the shoulder, then slipped out of the bed. Going into the bathroom, she bathed quickly. When she came out, Frank was lying in bed awake.

"You've always looked great in that towel," he said, adding coaxingly, "don't I get a good-morning kiss?"

Approaching the bed, she bent down only to have him capture her and pull her down fully on top of him.

She laughed and her lips found his. With the touch of ownership, his hands caressed her body and the kiss deepened.

"However, I think I like you even better without the towel," he growled and in the next instant it was on the floor.

"Don't you have a business we have to run?" she asked as his fingers gently massaged her thighs.

"Maryann has a key to the gate and the office and I just called her. She'll handle things."

"Sounds as if there's no rush for us to be anywhere," she said, kissing the hollow of his neck.

"No rush," he confirmed.

She felt his breathing becoming ragged. Abruptly freeing herself, she slipped off him. When he frowned questioningly, she smiled. "I don't think we need to have a sheet between us," she said, tossing it off and then lowering herself down beside him.

"Definitely don't need it," he agreed.

As she playfully nuzzled his neck, a mischievous smile curled her lips. "I was wrong about one thing."

Tilting her chin upward, he looked down into her face. "And what was that?"

"I told Ted that I'd learned that if something seemed too good to be true, then it most likely wasn't," she replied, combing a wayward lock of hair from his face with her fingers. "You, however, have proved me wrong."

"I'm amenable to providing you with a little more proof," he said, his hand moving leisurely along the curves of her body.

His touch left a trail of fire. "A little more proof does sound nice," she agreed huskily.

* * * * *

Silhouette Intimate Moments®